SAM, MERIAM, AND ME

A Novel

Baheej Khleif

Jameel Publishing
P.O. Box 1107, West Dundee, IL 60118
Orders or questions, contact:
email: JameelPublishing@aol.com
or Fax: 847-836-9811, or Tel: 847-207-0788

First Edition
Second Printing

ISBN: 978-0-9818225-0-1

MID-AMERICAN
PRINTING SYSTEMS, INC.

Printed in the United States by Mid-American Printing Systems, Inc., 400 South
Jefferson Street, Suite 300, Chicago, Illinois 60607. Tel: 312/663-4720

to

S A-K

BAHEEJ KHLEIF

The Author and the Story

This is a story about a love triangle between Sam, Meriam, and Me. The narrator is Sameer, born in Nazareth, in the Holy Land, and moved to the United States.

The triangle plays out on several levels: The personal between the three people, but also the levels of different cultures, and religions—Jewish, Christian, Moslem, Arab, American. We experience foods and celebrations, families, passion, and nostalgia. The novel explores relationships, conflicts, and histories—what if we could understand each other on a personal level? The style is prose and dialogue, almost lyrical.

Baheej Khleif was born in Nazareth—raised there and then went to Holland, and the USA to study. Has a Masters of Social Science from The International Institute of Social Studies at The Hague, Holland; a Ph.D. in sociology from the University of Colorado, Boulder; and a Masters in drama and fiction from Harvard University. He taught at the University of Wisconsin at LaCrosse and Copenhagen, Denmark; the University of Colorado at Boulder and Greeley; Worcester State in Massachusetts, and currently at Columbia College in Chicago.

Baheej Khleif was the first Director of the Arab-Jewish Cultural Center, Bet Hagefen, in Haifa, Israel. He speaks English, Arabic, Hebrew, and Dutch. Traveled widely in the USA, Scandinavia, continental Europe, South America, Asia, Morocco, Turkey, New Zealand, Canada, and Mexico. Visiting Scholar at the University of Tokyo. He has spoken widely at forums advocating peace. Recipient of a Massachusetts Arts Council grant to establish Theater Now, a project to encourage creativity; and a Ford Foundation Grant for graduate studies in Holland. The staged reading of his play at Columbia College, Chicago, The Wailing Wall, was supported by a grant from the Lilly Foundation. He writes fiction, drama, and fables.

ACKNOWLEDGEMENTS

Members of the Barrington Arts Council Writers group especially Gene Kimmet, Diane Kostick, Thomas P. Thomas, Natalie Pepa, George Pezdirtz, Tamara Tabel, Amanda Richards, Catherine Quigg, Janet Souter, Jerry Souter; colleagues at Worcester State in Massachusetts and the Last Friday of the Month Club especially Donna Joss, Ken Gibbs, Najib Saliba, Jeff Roberts, and Sandy Paracer; colleagues at Columbia College, Chicago, especially Steve Asma, Lisa Brock, Joan Erdman, Louis Silverstein, Janina Ciezaldo, Andrew Causey, and Oscar Valdez; Harvard University dramatic arts program, Sue Schopf, Robert Brustein, David Wheeler, Jeremy Geidt, Mark Leib. The University Club of Chicago and club Librarian, Despina Damolaris. All for their interest and support. Beth Fudala for her expertise in typing the manuscript. Michelle Britton for her photograph. My parents, Bassem Khleif and Naifeh Warwar Khleif. My beloved grandmother, Leah Warwar. My brothers, Bud, Suhail, and Waleed. My children, Leah, Rod, Al, and Joe. And to my wife Susan for her love.

SAM, MERIAM, AND ME

CHAPTER 1

The early buds of maple trees spread pink haze, and Boston ferns shake themselves out of winter hibernation. Night crawlers are crushed crossing the roads, to the delight of the robins. Nature repeats its vicious cycles. It's spring, and stress for some is pleasure for others.

Every day I walk three miles to the Oasis Restaurant in Cambridge, Massachusetts, where I work as a cook. How sad that on this cheery morning I should be thinking of leaving my wife, Christine, moving out.

At the Oasis, I find Sam, the owner, busy inspecting his looks in the mirrors of the dining room.

"Have you ever moved?" I ask him.

"Ten times as a student, three times with my divorces," he says chewing gum. Sam talks about divorce with the same detached tone a waiter might use to place an order -- two salads, light on lemon, and one coffee.

"Then you understand what I'm going through."

"There's nothing to it," Sam says, straightening his tie. "Take an eighteen footer, hundred dollar deposit, fifty dollars insurance. There's nothing to it."

"Eighteen footer?"

"Truck, of course, Sameer. We don't use camels for transport anymore. Seriously, we move all the time. There's nothing to it." Sam shrugs it off, avoiding the emotional issue.

"But I got used to my place," I say. "I like its crackling floor, its smell, its light. I hate to move, new neighbors, introductions. Last time I said, 'My name is Sameer,' a woman asked, 'Do you have a nickname?' I've barely dug my roots in. I can't stand my marriage, but I hate to move out. I live at a crossroad of indecision."

"You're sentimental and it's not good for business. See those customers in the corner? They ordered hummus with olive oil. Add red paprika. Get with it, man. Yesterday you served soup with a fork. God knows what you'll do today."

"Yes, sir," I say, joking. "Customers are our bread and butter."

"For God's sake, forget about the move. What are you trying to do, bankrupt me or something? Stop by later at my place and have a drink with us. I'll be your shrink. Would you trust yourself on the couch of a Jewish shrink?"

"I might as well. After all, you trust your restaurant in the hands of an Arab cook." Both of us laugh at the twist in our destinies.

That day I fix the hummus to perfection. There are no complaints, customers are pleased. The cash register rings excitedly, Sam beams. For a while, I forget about the problem of moving out. Sam has never invited me to his house before.

Curiosity has the effect of local anesthesia – curiosity numbs the rest of me. Sam often mentions his wife, Meriam but I've never met her. He separates his work from his home almost ruthlessly.

Soon after work I find myself standing at Sam's door.

"Here's my patient," he introduces me to Meriam.

"Sameer, Sam talks a lot about you."

"What do you Arabs drink?" Sam interrupts.

"Just a glass of camel milk," I say playing his game. "Make it heavy on Scotch with a bit of water."

2

"Ah, right away."

We sit facing each other on Danish furniture. Meriam sits next to me, her arms stretched along the back of the couch. Sam opposite.

"Sam told me you're headed for a difficult separation."

"Is there an easy one?" I ask.

"Five years from now you'll relate to your ex-wife like Early American furniture at the Museum of Fine Arts, all in the basement, past and forgotten," Sam blurts out.

Sam likes to be tough, sound tough, talk tough. He's short, stocky with the strongest jaws ever attached to a face. His eyes frown, flicker, and change with every move or word.

"Tell us something about yourself," Meriam says smiling.

Americans like to put people at ease by asking them about themselves. Back home we fold the self in; here we unfold it.

This is the moment I usually dread. Something about myself. What people want to know, and whether they care to know it, always puzzles me. A bit about myself invariably is sandwiched in conversation with new people. I have developed a short answer for the occasion. "Nothing much to say, really, nothing very exciting."

Before I can answer, Meriam adds, "I understand you're from Nazareth. Sam said you're moving out of your apartment and it's very difficult for you?" Meriam looks at me questioning, shifting in my direction, her right knee exposed under her corduroy skirt.

"It's a marriage of five years disintegrating faster than a piece of feta cheese. I seem to operate with partial vision. My choices waiver between self-deception and total ignorance." I sound vague because I find it difficult to discuss Christine. I love her and still respect her privacy.

"He talks like a philosopher," Sam shouts from the kitchen. "Sometimes I forget I'm in the restaurant business, just a rabbi sitting in a yeshiva with a problem student."

3

Sam doesn't fool me. I always get his serious answers out of context and unannounced. Three days from now, while I'm preparing a big order of stuffed green peppers, baba ghannouj, salads, and Arabic coffee, Sam will be saying, "About your choices, between total ignorance and self-deception, it's a lot of baloney to think that life has only two choices." He'll put the dilemma to rest, at least in his own mind.

"How about some cheese, "Meriam says smiling, and walks to the kitchen. I'm struck by the lightness of her movements.

As the evening unfolds, we talk about friendship and the constraints of making friends in a foreign country. I talk about myself and they listen. Maybe they'll suggest what I have already decided. That's usually the best form of advice. I feel warm and invited. The glow of human warmth touches me. I feel the surge of a tear. Don't be a bloody fool, I tell myself. If one tear rolls out of your eyes, you'll never live it down with Sam.

"Sameer is taking classes. Who ever heard of a cook doing that? People don't know their place anymore," Sam says laughing.

"No, I left school to work and save money. I'm only taking a writing class at night. So far we've only been talking, drinking, and praising each other's work."

"We can't take criticism," Meriam says. "It's an American trait. But look at the Japanese, they can't even say, 'No.' You have to coat criticism in sugar like medicine."

The telephone rings. It's for Sam. "Something came up," he says as he rushes out of the house. He insists that I stay and talk with Meriam.

He leaves us alone. An Arab would never leave his wife in the company of another man. Arabs believe in deep friendship and trust, but they never overestimate human nature.

Left alone with Meriam, I feel more comfortable looking at her face, with her wide, clear and green eyes. Looking at her eyes, I don't think I can tell a lie. I can only avoid the issue.

Meriam does not announce, as many Jewish friends have, "You're the first Arab I've met." I like that. I don't want to carry the responsibility of representing my race, performing a one-man show.

About Sam's rushing out, Meriam simply says, "Sam never overcame his parents' poverty. He's busy making money, making up for it."

I tell Meriam about my attachment to my parents. "A child is like a spiritual yo-yo," I say. "We spin away but jump back to the hand that threw us."

"You should write about yourself," she says. "What does Sameer mean in Arabic?"

I hesitate, for it means a good companion.

"Tell me about your writing class. I was thinking of taking one myself," she says.

"Students write from their own lives and often about their failures, suicide, rejections and drugs. A woman from Alaska writes about nature, moose, grass, lakes and mountains. She weaves her memories into breathtaking landscapes and wild animals. When I read her writing I feel I'm inhaling clean air in the mountain tops of Alaska. One student said, 'if you write about women, you should be able to describe their pubic hair.' My values were challenged. Is a crude picture of human reality art?"

"We never answered that question at Smith," Meriam says, moving her long chestnut hair from one side of her shoulder to the other. "Do you write candidly about moving out?"

"I'm sure my pen is biased."

"You never answered my question about your separation." Her eyes are bright with curiosity.

"Can you imagine an olive tree that is dry and dead except for one green branch? Every time I look at the twisted dry trunk I feel sad, remembering how full of life and love it used to be. Well, that's my marriage now. Every time I see Christine, I try to cling to the single green branch. I don't understand why intimacy dries out. Stale mustiness can even crawl into the sacred corners of the heart. Gifts given in love can become angry and bitter in separation."

Time slips smooth and fast.

Toward midnight Sam returns. Standing at the door, clasping his hands heartily, he says, "I know a place where you can find answers to all your questions. Go to the Boston Library and start reading the authors alphabetically!"

"Sam threatens to do just that when he retires," Meriam says laughing.

"Some people need answers in the beginning, I need them at the end." Sam sits by Meriam and pulls her close to him.

Meriam looks at her watch. "My, it's already midnight. I hope you earned a living for the three of us," she tells Sam.

I feel strange about being included.

"By the way," Meriam asks, "have you found an apartment?"

"No," I answer.

Human warmth is magic. I leave Sam and Meriam feeling elated. The paradox of it all. I can hear Sam telling Meriam, "Just think of the fate of Sameer. Comes all the way to the U.S. to get rid of the Israelis and gets stuck with two Jews instead."

He's right, of course. Destiny does have a perverse sense of humor. The more I think about being a Palestinian, the more I feel sad how my people are trapped in history, our destinies caught up in the wheels of political events mostly beyond our personal control.

CHAPTER 2

The first whiff of night air brings the chill of hard decisions. My head throbs with oppressive thoughts. For every "you are right to divorce Christine," a "you are not" rushes to the fore. Thoughts drum wildly inside me. Thoughts and counter-thoughts rage.

Meriam's phrase "difficult separation" snags my heart. I try to pick the real reason for my separation. Should it be big? What about trivial reasons like an irritating twitch of a nervous small finger, a frown on her face. Petty things erode strong relationships. I have seen pretty gypsy moths demolish the beautiful green foliage of giant oak trees. They excrete it like dirty black hail to the ground.

Truth masquerades in a constant kaleidoscope. Even a gypsy moth turns into a dormant cocoon before it bursts again into a moth. I try to unmask the problem. I love Christine. I flooded her with flowers until I could not see her face, with candles until I burnt my fingers. I did not see the cracks in the mosaic. A worshiper never questions deity.

Christine was racing with success and I waited at the finish line, an admiring spectator for her degrees and awards. Christine held to me. She still does. Me, uprooted, turned waiter, turned cook, turned...I have to stop this. If there is anything I cannot tolerate, it's my own sense of self-pity.

I am waiting for a convincing voice to tell me, "Sameer, you are right to divorce. You are justified. You'll not regret it." But there is no voice. Christine does not suffer regrets. She plods on her path, not once allowing herself to doubt her own integrity. I, on the other hand, rock on a roller coaster of moral doubt.

Christine is slender and brunette. No, Christine is vicious and brunette, but her long hair is such a part of it. For a whole decade I have observed her two-hour ritual, every two days, shampooing, then curling, then under the dryer, then combing. Women touch themselves more often than men.

I open the locked door to our apartment.

"Is that you?" Christine calls in a baby-like voice from the bedroom. She never leaves her bed after going to sleep.

"Yes, it's me," I murmur, heading to the kitchen.

I open the refrigerator, stretch my hand to find anything salty, hoping for black olives or cheese. The kitchen is zealously exorcised of starch, sweets and fat. I find an apple and crackers. Christine only keeps thin crackers, wafer-types, like the ones you get in communion. Their potency is spiritual. There is some celery and carrots. Evening is the time when I miss my own cooking. I crave a piece of Arabic bread, brown and puffed the way it comes from the baker's furnace, with some homemade apricot jam.

I enter our bedroom. I get a kiss. I'm amazed how kisses have become perfunctory in marriage while so much of my passion is running loose in the house.

Christine's eyes are half-open, her expression set in thin lips and high, sharp cheeks. Her narrow eyes, once shining with adoration, now look from a distance. I tell myself in pain, not one tender tissue has been left. Her face doesn't smile, it merely wrinkles, cold and rational.

"I want to tell you something, and I bet you don't even care," Christine says.

"I do care. I do," I rush to say.

"You don't even want to know," she closes her eyes and turns over, facing the wall. I have gone through this scene so many times. The anticipation makes me cold.

Christine has surrendered to anxieties about her teaching and her diet. I occupy her war zone. For years we sat facing each other at the dining room table discussing her weight, which in its most extreme violation increased from 112 to 114 pounds. Amazing how a clear mind gets entangled in guilt the size of two cookies.

8

"Of course I care. I'm just tired."

"Well, don't overwork. Don't stay up so late."

"What happened to you?" I ask her again.

"Never mind."

"Come on now. What happened?"

"If you cared, you'd stay at home."

"I visited Sam."

"Oh, did he invite you alone?"

"You're always busy in the evening, either writing or sleeping." My mind flashes to evenings and weekends with Christine working, writing; papers crumbled on the floor. Christine without emotion, no time for marriage, no time for us. Arguing about taking a break, doing something together, but not succeeding.

"You don't care if I publish anything. You have a secure job. You can always be a chef."

I fear the sweetness of the evening spent with Sam and Meriam will dissipate, driven away like early morning fog.

"I want to talk to you."

"You know that I'm half asleep now. Why are you trying to make me feel guilty?"

I think we have serious things to discuss," I blurt out, regretting the poor timing.

"Oh, that's really not nice. Do you know what time it is?"

I walk to the living room. I hate being there alone. I look at some newspapers then go back to the kitchen. I start eating anything I can find, partly out of hunger, partly out of bitterness. I hear Christine's mumbling from a distance. She walks into the living room carrying her pillow and blanket, dressed in one of my shirts barely covering the tops of her shapely bare legs. She stretches on the sofa.

"Tell me your serious thing. What are you up to this time? You woke me up," she says wrapping herself in the blanket.

This is the wrong time for serious conversation. We have a long history of tense encounters at such times, and the consequences can be grave.

Christine looks fragile and sleepy on the couch. I feel like an executioner.

"I'm sorry, I didn't mean to wake you up. I'll carry you to bed." I love to carry her to bed. I like her helplessness in my arms.

The next day we sit facing each other. Christine is pouring out all of her day on me, a detailed replay of everything that happened or crossed her mind. With her eyes fixed on me, she talks of Jordan Marsh shoes, their heels and style this year, of the comments she has made in her classes and the problems she had with some over-anxious students. I know if I interrupt her she will tell me, "Don't ask me how my day went if you don't want to listen. If I bore you so much, why don't you say it?"

I wait for a natural pause in her monologue. I hold my chair tight then say, "I want a divorce."

I try to freeze my face in order not to betray my doubts. I fought for the survival of my marriage with fits, love notes and affection. But what is left is a leafless tree with one green branch pleading for survival. "Mother Nature," I heard the branch pleading inside me. "What about all the seasons, all the warm sunshines and storms we've spent together?" And with the predictable reaction of nature, I heard myself replying, "That's life and death." My life is in brutal harmony with nature.

"You must be joking." Christine's confidence is cold and firm.

"No, I'm not."

"Why do this? Are you crazy or something?" A faint twitch flashes on her face. The first emotion she has shown in a long time.

"No, I've thought a lot about it."

"Then you must be mad."

"I don't think so." Short replies. Words would only trip me up.

"You want to throw everything away, down the drain?" A faint fear surfaces in her voice.

Sensing her fears and pain crumbles my resistance. Seeing the shadows of her anxiety, I am struck by panic like a trapeze artist losing control, afraid of my own fall. I lost my home country and my parents across the Atlantic. I wanted to escape tradition, and now I am on the verge of losing my wife. I hope I am right. I sit anticipating a hailstorm.

"Are you going to give up everything?" She focuses her eyes on my soul.

"Yes."

"What about our plans to go to Europe?"

"Well…"

"What are you going to tell my parents? And your family?"

At some point all language translates itself in belief, then into action.

"Do you have a place already?"

"No."

"Maybe you should take a vacation and think it over."

Later in the evening Christine says, "Maybe we can live in separate rooms, even apartments, but stay married. Still later, says, "It's okay with me if you want to go out at night. You don't have a girlfriend, do you?"

As a last resort, she says, "Maybe we'll just separate."

At this point of her slow retreat I feel the saddest. Her defeat is painful to me.

"No, Christine," I say in a cold voice that chills my own ears. "Our marriage strangled our intimacy. I'm getting out of it." I'm too cowardly to tell her more.

She's crying. In the past Christine always registered a knock-out at this round. I am demolished by the sight of her tears. All her face becomes expressive, all of it cries. She stands up, goes to the bedroom and slams the door. An act like that, in the past, would be followed by my pious attempts to reconcile. Otherwise, I'd be accused, "You really don't give a damn if I cry myself to death, alone."

I hold tight to my chair and stay in the living room long enough to invoke fears and nightmares about what Christine could do to herself and me. At last I hear her coming out, her face dry but pained.

"Let's talk about it," she says softly.

I realize that my words are putting things in motion. I collapse in the chair, listening sadly to the effect, to the impact and direction.

"I want to be the one suing you for divorce."

"Fine," I answer, with a sense of awe, finalizing a fateful deal.

CHAPTER 3

Does surgery ever heal? I have passed by trees soon after their branches were cut, sap flowing over their trunks. A month later, the scars were dry and had a deathly color. I often wondered if the trees remembered those branches that had bent lovingly over the road. I would whisper, "What became of those branches?" The trees would not answer.

You always remember a home you lost. How could I forget my hometown, Nazareth? Nazareth is where the local liquor, Arak, is called Holy Water. It's where mothers rock the cradle with arms as strong as Goliath and stand behind their children, firm as oak trees. Nazareth is where all the senses are exuberant -- for sunset, for spring. It's where figs, grapes and cactus fruits are grown and eaten at home, Biblical lentil dishes, hot dough dipped in honey. Sensations of belonging still surge within me, even with any mention of the famous Nazarene.

Nazareth comes to me every day—when I see a beautiful apple, a flower, a bunch of grapes, or when a mother nurses her baby with tenderness and attention. I have been here several years, but when customers ask me where I'm from, I know they're not asking about Massachusetts.

Sam's Oasis doesn't attract Palestinians or Middle Eastern types, despite it's name. He had an amateur painter decorate it with lots of palm trees that appear to be standing on their toes. He claims the painter never saw anything except oak trees and strawberry patches his entire life.

Restaurants develop unique vibes and attract their own special clientele. As Sam says, "You can't discuss politics in fast food restaurants."

The Oasis attracts two kinds of customers -- those who find everything "bizarre," and those who say, "drives me crazy" about a wide range of things from high prices, to people, to heavy rain. These two types never mix. They sit at different tables and sometimes watch each other, and when they get bored they watch me.

A few days after my visit with Sam and Meriam, Sam asks me abruptly, "Have you found a place yet?"

"No."

"Why don't you move in with us?"

"Move in with you?" I repeat.

"Yes, why not? We'll have the Security Council meetings in our den. Next time my bigot brother-in-law launches an attack on the Arabs, at least the Palestinian point of view will be represented." Sam laughs heartily.

Sam chose the busiest time of the day to shock me. Orders are piled high, the grill is packed.

Deep inside me I think how absurd it is that I should end up with Sam's home address in Newton. Isn't Newton called Little Israel? It might as well be Tel-Aviv: c/o Sam Weinstein, Tel-Aviv.

Seeing my surprise, Sam adds, "We've had people stay with us before. Last year our friend, David, was here for six months. Great company! You'd take Esther's room."

"Who is Esther?" I ask.

"First child from my first marriage. She only uses the room between broken love affairs. Maybe it will help her find a husband if her room is occupied again," Sam says laughing. "Esther has been going to college forever. I don't know what she's looking for."

"The search is a state of mind," I say mostly to myself.

"Ah—search? You haven't seen the courses she takes and the textbooks she buys. Now she's taking Human Sexual Awareness. You'd think they're preparing her for a career in the red light district." Sam's eyes twinkle with amusement. "That man's hunger is a state of mind," Sam whispers to me, pointing to an obese customer. "He ordered kibbee, tahini, stuffed squash, and custard. He'll probably stop at Burger King afterward and get two double Whoppers for dessert."

Should I move in with Sam and Meriam? It's a question of personal history. Should a Palestinian end his wandering in a Jewish household?

"And don't think it's for free," Sam says, interrupting my thoughts. "One seventy five for rent and heat, five for garage, and lots of snow shoveling in the winter."

Only temporarily. I'll move in with Sam and Meriam, then I'll move again.

CHAPTER 4

I want a clean exit from marriage. Is there a clean exit after years of love and anger? It takes me all summer to face the move.

Finally, I rent a U-Haul, an ugly one with a clumsy square frame and nauseating dampness seeping from its insides. I drive to Belmont, the radio moaning folk songs, and the U-Haul rattling scandalously behind me, "Divorce...Divorce...Divorce..." to every passer-by. I feel I am driving a U-Haul/hearse combination. Burial time. I will take my belongings and the casket will be shut amid tears, sobs, and flying furniture. How strange human nature is. I am still eager to see Christine. Judas' last supper ritual.

I find Christine in a new dress, her make-up impeccable and a red rose in her hair.

"You can't park the U-Haul on the lawn. You'll destroy the grass."

It's not exactly the passionate or tragic farewell I envisioned.

"It's raining heavily outside and the distance will be incredible," I tell her.

"That's your problem."

The dumb U-Haul becomes the target. We always fight on side-tracks, terrified by the heart of the matter.

I start to collect my belongings. I feel the way one must feel moving into a nursing home, leaving all that counts behind. I throw my clothes into suitcases, but carefully pack the letters from my family. I rattle away with an almost empty U-Haul.

Does moving in with Sam and Meriam smack of betrayal and really change who I am? I don't want to tackle that, but it burns in my veins.

I move into Esther's room, a beautiful corner room that captures the sunset and overlooks a pond, an unbelievable dream.

I go to sleep relieved but have a nightmare. My head jolts, my eyes open to the total darkness of the room, to vast loneliness. I turn the lights on and try to recapture my nightmare. I was angry with my mother, screaming, "Damn it, Mother, I want to talk to my father. Where is my father? Who is our father?" I spend the rest of the night apologizing to Mother, but I cannot convince myself it was only a dream.

In the morning I get a glimpse of Meriam in a long olive robe, stepping gently over a thick tan rug. "Have some coffee, Sameer. How did you sleep? You can help yourself to anything you want in the kitchen."

I tell her the last thing a cook wants is to stand in his own kitchen. Sam, propelled by great energies, is already gone. I dress fast and walk to work.

When I enter the Oasis he stands beaming by the cash register. "Meriam is planning to have you speak to her Hadassah group."

"Hadassah group?"

"A wealthy Jewish women's organization."

"No, no. What could I tell them?"

"Exchange recipes," Sam says with a mischievous smile.

I shake my head at the mention of Hadassah. Sam notices my anxiety. Two hours later he says, "Don't worry, Sameer, the Jews are not in the business of conversion. It just isn't profitable. We leave that to Catholic priests in Africa."

I laugh, feeling at ease. What Sam says is true.

The first week in Newton I walk around the neighborhood in a daze—a frightened animal shaken out of hibernation. I feel like running back to Christine. I miss my daily preoccupation with her. But, I don't go back. I suddenly remember the first time my parents took me to school in Nazareth, when I ran home after them.

The new environment in Esther's room asserts itself. I hit my head on unshut drawers. I bruise my body on unfamiliar corners. Finally, I open my eyes to my surroundings. I am living with Sam and Meriam.

I eye the <u>Encyclopedia Judaica</u> every time I pass it in the corridor, but I never open it. In my room, <u>The Palestinian Question</u>, by Edward Said glitters with bolder light. I think with amusement maybe I'll give Sam a copy of the Bible.

I have a drawing of Christ that a painter friend drew in the sixties. I call him my Hippie Christ. In it, Christ appears impoverished, real, bearded, with the clear look of a vegetarian in his eyes. I get up around three A.M. and hang him on the wall.

When Sam sees Christ the next day, he points to him and says, "Ah hah, that's the Jewish connection."

Loneliness is Thanksgiving followed by Christmas followed by New Year's. Stabs of pain.

I spend endless hours talking to Christine on the phone. I call about her work and talk about her days. I miss her.

One evening I take a bottle of extra dry champagne and go to see her. On the surface, her world still looks the same. The list of items to be done the next day is in the same place on the kitchen counter. I exit two hours later, pained at the ease with which she lets me leave. I initiated my own separation, but it's the paradox of love and hate.

I tell Sam about my visit to Christine. He finds the champagne idea amusing. "The cooks I had before you drank beer after work," he chuckles. "And never with their wives, let alone their ex-wives."

On my day off, Sam and Meriam invite me to have coffee and strudel. Meriam is an engaging listener. I am waiting for her to tell me more about herself. I feel the anticipation of getting to know her. Sam sits on the rug glancing through newspapers. Meriam faces me on the couch, asking about my writing class.

"Men are becoming sex objects, the dice are rolling back," I say. "Two women wrote about relationships that didn't go beyond crude sexual exploitation. The men in their stories, an architect in one and an engineer in another, were portrayed with nothing deeper than crude sexuality. Nothing spiritual or intellectual." Sam listens, amused by my story. "Maybe I'm overreacting," I say. "I mean, even when de Maupassant wrote about whores, he found more than crude sex."

"You haven't met American engineers!" Sam cackles.

"At last women's sexual fantasy is finding an expression," Meriam says. Her body, though relaxed, is still attentive. Her silence is warm, warm as her deep green eyes that create rings of warmth around Sam and me.

"I've given up trying to understand women," I laugh. "Men and women rotate in different orbits."

"I think you're absolutely right. We need a new story of creation," Sam interjects. "Adam's rib doesn't make sense anymore."

Meriam smiles. This time her smile is difficult to interpret.

CHAPTER 5

One day I get a notice from a probate court that it has finally allocated fifteen minutes for my divorce.

Courts are foreign to me, like hospitals and funeral homes. On the morning of our hearing, I meet Christine in court. The building is crowded with lawyers walking around like panthers. Christine looks beautiful and relaxed. She smiles at me, and I know there will be no scandal.

My lawyer whispers to me, "The judge is new." I look mystified. The lawyer adds between his teeth, "This judge is one of the governor's appointees."

We approach the bench. The judge is a red-haired man who smiles shyly at us. "Have you discussed this matter between you?"

"Yes," we answer.

"Okay," he says. "The agreements shall merge and survive." And he signs.

It takes only two minutes. No French guillotine could have done a cleaner job in a shorter time.

We kiss farewell, our marriage left behind in a folder with the clerk of the court.

I know I'll see Christine again. Merge and survive. The legal terms keep pounding in my head.

Sam, anticipating a gloomy cooking day, gives me the day off. I wanted this divorce to happen and it did. I try to track its beginning. A small act must have started it a long time ago. You move one stone and it starts a path.

The whole afternoon I live in the eye of the hurricane. I vow no more marriages. When the French revolutionaries finished killing the queen, they started killing each other. There is no target left but me.

By midnight I am drunk. I stop at Dunkin' Donuts on Route 30.

The place is empty. The waitress is sitting reading the Bible. I can't believe my eyes. She looks content.

"Are you interested in the Bible?" she asks.

She's a Jehovah's Witness and has found purpose in life at last. I believe her. She joins me in the booth and, with great contentment, relates stories from <u>Watch Tower</u>, a booklet Jehovah Witnesses distribute all over the country. She gives me a copy designed like a travel agent's guide to happiness. It says there is much more to life. She hands me another official publication called <u>Awake</u>.

In the morning, I show the publication to Sam. He glances at it and says, "They certainly need a name like that if they work the night shift." Sam is always kicking at hidden corners.

CHAPTER 6

Meriam finishes her introduction and hands me the microphone. I am left alone. I am facing her Hadassah group, all ready for lunch and the speaker, all consumed by social causes. I stammer, apologizing for my English.

"Palestine is a semantic problem," one woman provokes me. "It never existed."

"Why can't you sit together and talk together, live together? What is Palestine anyway?" another interrupts.

"How can I explain Palestine to you? My voice is charged with passion. I'll tell you about ecstasy instead. Ecstasy is simple. Ecstasy is life throbbing from juices of fruit trees in our garden in Nazareth. It's peeling a fresh fig and eating its succulent body. It's holding a cucumber with the earth heat still in its veins. Ecstasy is a garden we own in Palestine, now Israel, where my grandparents and ten centuries of blood relatives before them walked and still do."

I glance at Meriam. Her eyes expect the truth. It has to be my truth. "Ecstasy is…"

Hadassah questions pour over me. I see their pupils tighten and dim. They only see me as an Arab. I forget Christine. I forget being a cook.

I answer with a barrage of "what abouts…" Confiscation of lands, deportation, demolition of ancient Arab villages, wreckage of a natural order.

"Meriam drives me home. She touches me gently on the arm. "Sameer, you were great."

"I think I'm a mess," I say.

At home, Sam listens to Meriam's excited report and grins broadly. "A few more speeches and those old girls will match you with a Jewish American Princess so they can say, my son-in-law, the Palestinian."

Meriam laughs and serves us drinks. Beer for Sam, Scotch for me, Dubonnet for her. I drink a lot. Nostalgia mixes well with liquor.

"Ecstasy is peeling a fresh fig and eating its succulent body, that's what Sameer told them," Meriam says, looking at Sam.

"Mother started labor with me while up in a tree picking figs," I say. "Mother always added, smiling, 'I was very young, Sameer.'"

"Ecstasy is you, honey." Sam kisses Meriam on her bare arm. Meriam acknowledges his kiss gently by a caress and quickly says, "I haven't even seen a fig tree, Sameer. I feel deprived."

"We have them in our garden. Come visit us in Palestine."

"Israel, you mean," Sam retorts.

"Palestine," I insist with sweet obnoxiousness.

"Don't romanticize the fig tree," Sam says. "It has very small leaves. You'd be shocked by the anatomy of Adam and Eve. They must have been trendy dressers in the Garden of Eden. Of course, their descendants know it's the power of the act that counts, not the proportions."

"Your mind is occupied with sex and food," Meriam says, fondling his curly hair.

"They're both food. They're not far apart." Sam looks at me. "Sameer should know that. After all, you Arabs have an insatiable appetite for women."

"What about love?" I say. Sameer, you continue to be naive, I think to myself.

"You don't need love for either. All you need is the right approach and some musical background," Sam replies, pleased with himself.

"Sam, really," Meriam says.

"It's okay, we can talk in front of Sameer. He's our in-house goy," Sam says laughing.

"Sameer is our friend, not our in-house gentile, you silly thing." To stress her point, Meriam gives me an affectionate hug and quickly changes the topic. "You must have quite a beautiful garden."

"The pomegranates are the most beautiful, with the most regal flowers. In spring they burst out with a crown-shaped bud, an altar on fire. We have almond trees and apricots. During the summer we live outdoors. We sit in the shade of grape vines lifted up like a roof around our house."

"I grew up in Mattapan," Sam breaks in. "I was in the Zionist Youth Movement. At fourteen Alia was our dream, emigration to Israel."

"At fourteen? Oh, my God. I was weaving peaceful dreams. We had a false sense of security watching sunsets from the slopes of mountains surrounding Nazareth, writing poetry, and being deeply in love."

"And at sixteen?" Meriam asks.

"By then Israel was established. Most of the people were terrified when war erupted. It took us by surprise like an earthquake. People fled. Those refugees still treasure their keys and deeds to the land. What did you do at seventeen, eighteen?" I ask Sam.

"At eighteen I had to marry Sarah," Sam sighs, annoyed by the memory. "Oh yes. Then came Esther and Matt, as fast as an automatic sprinkler. Matt is okay, studying to become a rabbi at Hebrew Union."

"None of my brothers are studying to become rabbis," I try to kid Sam. "At eighteen, I was leading demonstrations against Israeli discrimination."

"At twenty I was moving out of my first marriage," Sam says.

"And Miri?"

"Miri. I like to be called Miri," she says. "I was sheltered in the groves of academe. I was at Smith busy reading D.H. Lawrence and James Joyce. When did you meet Jews for the first time?" she says, trying to change the focus of the conversation.

"The first foreigners I came across were engraved on Roman coins we dug up in our garden as children."

I always try to sit facing Meriam. She always manages to look me straight in the eyes. Meriam's eyes have a velvet effect, with dark eyelashes. With other women I look somewhere else. I may notice beautiful hair, be distracted by a curve of the body, a movement of the head, a tone of voice. But with Meriam it's her eyes.

Sam and Meriam never fight. Whenever Sam is cornered by a problem, he laughs his way out of it. I have a strange feeling Sam would like the three of us to grow closer.

CHAPTER 7

Man wants to grow roots, not be a tumbleweed. Life with Sam and Meriam radiates the right warmth from a stable earth. The trimmings become the focus. The small rituals, the coffee on Sunday. Meriam arranging the coffee table, silver, china with true blue delicate flowers over ornate green branches, French Limoges. The aroma of fresh espresso gushes out with the steam. One yellow rose or red carnation on the breakfast table. A few assorted cakes. And Meriam all gay and happy. Fitted shirt and fitted skirt calling from downstairs, "Sameer, Nazarenes are not supposed to work on Sunday."

I feel Meriam's human touch, her attention. I resist seeing more, but there is more to see. A mouth not wrinkled by meanness or bitterness. A body controlled not to overexpose its beauty. I better stop here.

Sam is always checking the <u>Boston Globe</u> to see if it's printing the Oasis ad correctly. The texture of this man is so varied. Sam at work, and Sam at home. At home, a furry purring strength. At work, a soft treading tiger, waiting for prey, centered on survival. Men and women surround him, fascinated - - men for his humor and energy, women for humor and masculinity.

While at home both of us orbit around Meriam. And Meriam, with subtle finesse, keeps us in harmony and in still motion. When Meriam pours coffee it acquires a human touch like a hug. We sip it, savor the espresso and the faint flavor of a thin lemon peel.

"You should ask Sameer to read your fortune from your coffee cup," Sam says.

"Oh, Sameer—you must," Meriam implores.

I remember Mother sitting among her women friends, all hushed. One anxious woman asking her, "Tell us, Um-Sameer, Mother of Sameer, what do you see?" Mother, restrained and quiet, turning the cup slowly with three fingers, saying, "You had a sad week. You are getting a letter, a gift, or news. Maybe in one week, maybe one month, maybe one year, I can't tell." The women store every utterance of fortune in their memories. "See that fish," Mother tells them, "That's a bundle of fortune." For more severe destinies, "Snakes are all around. I see lots of jealousy and envy." And the women always shake their heads puzzled and agreeing. They always side with the unknown over what they know. But when concerns about questions of passion overflow - - does he love me or does he not, Mother nods for me to leave the room.

"When you're through drinking the coffee, you tip the cup over like this to dry." I turn Meriam's cup over and lay it on the edge of the saucer. "Mother reads fortunes only for privileged friends," I say. I look intently into shapes of the sediment formed inside the cup. "I see you confronting a woman. She looks angry and hostile."

Sam comes to look at the cup.

"You look firm and quiet," I say. "There are two trips ahead of you. You seem undecided. Both look like strange places, but close to each other."

"I'll be damned, Sameer, sure enough we're talking about the Canary Islands or Nova Scotia, but they're in two different corners of the globe," Sam says. "Fortune-tellers should know their geography better than that."

"Sam, keep quiet. Wait until your turn. Is there no privacy in this house?" Meriam nudges him away from her cup. "It's true, we're debating where to spend our vacation," she adds smiling.

"Except for that, I see lots of good signs, for letters, gifts. It's a beautiful cup."

"Thank you, Sameer. Now who is that woman showing in my cup?"

"I recognize the woman, but I don't say. Christine's long hair is loosened furiously down the side of the cup, it looks like an Aegean vase with a war goddess sketched on its surface.

"It's my turn," Sam says, handing me his empty cup. "Is there money in my cup?"

"C'mon, I only read to believers," I say. Sam's cup has lots of money signs.

"The Palestinians were busy reading their fortunes while the Jews were planning to take over Palestine. Nobody seems to have seen that in their coffee cups," Sam says triumphantly.

For once I agree with Sam on politics. Our fortune-tellers were blind. We were blind. We stayed inside the fences of our daily lives. In those days we only saw each other. We felt secure because we were the majority in our own land.

Why is Christine appearing to me in Meriam's cup? With Meriam and Sam, I almost forget her. Christine's memory is seductive. Seduction is half vision, half anticipation. I wonder how she is managing. I feel a lump in my throat wondering whether she already has a lover.

CHAPTER 8

Once a month Sam visits his competitors, "a tour to the battlefield," as he puts it. He's dressed in his best and has assembled his staff of five waitresses, two assistant cooks, and me.

"In our business, nerves are important," he says. "We have to keep those guys on their toes." Today Sam wears his religious hat. "Let's go sample some Jewish food, Sameer."

I put on my bright Oasis shirt with the Oasis logo, and we leave. "I'll know from the way they act how well their restaurants are doing," Sam says.

We enter a competing restaurant on Brattle Street. "Cohen, meet my chef, Sameer," Sam introduces me to the owner.

"What's the matter, Sam, coming at this hour? Are you selling out?" Cohen asks Sam jokingly.

"No, we're packed. We thought we'd find empty seats here," Sam quips back.

"Well, if you get tired of working for Sam, now you know where to come," Cohen announces.

"You'd be leaving a reformed Jew for an orthodox one," Sam chuckles. "And an extreme Zionist," he adds between his teeth.

Sam chooses the most prominent table where he can sit and watch people. "The best alternative to a sidewalk café," he says. "People put on their best show when they eat in public. Buddha says man is a menagerie of hungry animals."

"That sounds a bit out of context," I say. "Didn't Buddha say it may be better for man to fast because he can't satisfy all those animals?"

"Well, Buddha didn't grow up in a Jewish kitchen," Sam says. "See that woman? She barely opens her mouth, afraid somebody might steal a secret. And the way that guy is pounding the ketchup bottle, you'd think it's his mother-in-law. See how people center on babies and neglect their partners, see the way their feet wiggle under the table in intense excitement. I tell you, Sameer, some people go to the theatre, but I go to restaurants. Look at the hands - - the chubby, the elegant, the bony and frazzled. Look at the way they hold a sandwich, all the fingers poised to look genteel."

"Watch out for those hearty customers who want to eat their dollar's worth - - bread, sugar, butter and all," Sam warns. "When those guys are through, you're lucky if they leave salt and pepper in the shakers." Sam's eyes flicker with mischief. Then, in a sudden change of topic, he confides, "At the Oasis, the waitresses are crazy about you."

"Me?" I say surprised. "I wish I could read women better."

"Oh, no. If you mix business with sex, you'd get a bad hangover. Now, business and politics, that's fine." Sam looks thoughtful and adds, "Why don't you invite some of your friends to the Oasis? I mean Palestinians. Arabs. I'd like to have them as customers."

The idea sounds funny, but I don't think much about it.

The mention of sex brought Christine to my mind, all naked and absorbed. Making love with Christine was like going to church. I always paid at the end of mass, a bit of my soul, a concession to a demand. Man rarely sees the whole woman; he completes her shape in his mind. The idea of finding another partner is discouraging.

Returning home, we find Meriam reading, her hand casually snug in her hair at the side of her head.

"I've been wined and dined, poorly of course," Sam announces. "My Oasis remains at the top of the list. I give it five stars. Now I've got some other business," Sam adds and leaves.

A flash of curiosity grips me about Sam's other business.

"I had a surprise visit," Meriam says. "Christine stopped by." Sensing my anxiety, she adds, "We talked mainly about literature and your writing."

"Why did she come?" I ask. A scout spying on the defense lines before the attack. Christine is collecting clues.

"Christine is worried about how you're managing. I think she still loves you."

I looked around to observe changes in the room, detect echoes of Christine's visit. "Tell me more."

"She's very attractive."

I fumble, not knowing how to take a compliment for my ex-wife. I know how perfect she can look, her skirt length just right.

"Christine could not stop talking about you," Meriam interrupts my wild fantasy. "She told me that without your patience and support she would never have finished her studies. I didn't realize Christine had a Ph.D.," she adds softly.

The very mention of her degree sprouts acid memories. Years of typing, tearing, and tensions at home, with me in the target zone.

"Oh...yes...she's overeducated for me." I don't tell Meriam that I miss Christine's intellect.

"Sameer, its culture that counts, not titles or degrees." Meriam folds Durrell's <u>Balthazar</u> and puts it reverently on her lap and stares at me warmly. "Durrell writes in this book, 'love is a liquid fossil'. Christine loves you." Meriam tries to diffuse the sudden tide of emotions.

"If love is a liquid fossil, then what is God?" I ask, not comprehending my own question.

CHAPTER 9

I bounce back to Christine, partly out of habit, partly out of curiosity.
I call first - - afraid of surprises. She invites me to dinner.

"Come in," she welcomes me like a guest at the door. "What shall I
fix you to drink?"

In a quick glance I see that she has filled all the empty spaces.
Bursts of new colors everywhere. Marimekko curtains with bigger-than-
life lotus flowers. Lotuses are my favorite. New red rug. I detect a cozy
light from the bedroom door. New dress. The couches are moved facing
each other. On the coffee table a stack of folders neatly arranged with a
note to herself—"give to Sameer."

She sits relaxed and smiling. The smells of sautéed eggplant, fried
meat, and toasted pine nuts fill the room. "After I left, you learned how
to cook!" I kid her.

I'm anxious to hear about her visit to Meriam. "Sorry I wasn't there
when you came by," I say.

"Oh, yes, I'll tell you about that…but don't let me forget those files.
I made you a copy of all our documents." Christine follows her own list
of priorities. She routinely copies everything that gets into her hands.
In medieval times she would have been a monk endlessly copying papal
correspondence.

The only thing she can't copy is me, and I am not sure she's accepted
that. In the next century Vatican monks will probably use a cloning
machine. Actually I like this quality in her. She can find a canceled
check within a few minutes. If I ask her about the first play we saw, she
gives me the program from the play with the stub of the ticket stapled to
it. Christine has her eyes open for all the things I don't see.

I have decided to enjoy the evening. I lean back on the couch, cross
my legs, and light my pipe. The dinner is superb. The recipe is my
mother's. I translated it for Christine.

I enjoy listening to Christine drift through her stream of consciousness about spy novels she reads before she falls asleep, about problems in her research, and about the recent increase in suicide. She looks steadily into my eyes and relates to me names of writers and findings. She talks about segments of the population that commit the most suicide. I sit awed by her brass metal mind, listening to its pure clicks, abstracting suicidal tragedy into cohorts.

Then, without changing her tone of voice, she asks, "Did you write your family about us? You know my family is shocked and so are all our friends."

"They only see one side of the moon," I say, trying to avoid the topic.

On our first meeting, her father got drunk. His eldest daughter marrying a foreigner and an Arab was too much for him. He spent the evening bragging about Christine's accomplishments in high school. Later, her parents introduced me to their friends at a huge cocktail party at their country club. The friends carried drinks and broad smiles and circled around me, an exotic animal in a touch-and-go encounter.

"I've gone through our albums. I'm keeping the ones from Yellowstone. I made you copies of the good ones—but you look good in all your pictures."

"Thank you," I say, always expecting a setback shortly after a compliment. I am ready to hear about Meriam.

"I met Sam in the most unlikely place."

"Sam?" I ask with astonishment.

"Yes, on campus."

"He never told me he takes classes."

"No—as a guest speaker for B'nai Brith."

Christine shows me an announcement for a talk on "The Future of Israel" with Sam's picture on it. "Sam Weinstein, sole survivor of a family of four in a concentration camp. Lived in Israel and now the

U.S. A leading figure in Jewish organizations." At the bottom of the announcement, I read: "Presently married to Meriam Strauss, a member of a prominent business family."

Sam never mentioned his past. Does he want to protect our friendship? To think of the agony Sam's family went through in a concentration camp and he's still able to laugh. I am optimistic about my own fate and feel a tide of affection for Sam and Meriam.

"Did you know all this about Sam?" Christine asks. She doesn't like hints. She likes to register her points in black and white.

"Did you attend his talk?" I ask back.

"No, but I ran into him. He's funny. He told me he originally hired you to establish some balance in his ideology. He invited me to stop by and see Meriam."

I am intrigued.

Christine serves the dessert, pecan pie. If it was the apple for Adam, it was pecan pie for me. She came with a pecan pie on our second date, her grandmother's Southern recipe. Christine looks at me with lit eyes. "Guess what? I have the orange striped sheets you love on the bed." She moves over and sits on my lap.

"Is this a proposition?" I ask, teasing.

"Oh Sameer…honey."

We go to the bedroom. The light is soft; the striped sheets are inviting and fresh. Christine's body feels familiar. I hug her close for all the yearnings I have. I lie on the bed vulnerable, my defenses swept away.

Christine walks to the kitchen, brings two glasses of wine, and then says, "Well, frankly I wonder about your plans. How long are you going to stay with Sam and Meriam?"

"I live there," I say with short simplicity.

"Do you want to give your address, Sameer c/o Sam Weinstein, to your Arab friends?"

I stammer, avoiding the question.

"I didn't force this dilemma on you. You got yourself into it."

I surprise myself, telling Christine, "Sam is not a political dilemma to me. Sam is my friend."

"And Meriam?"

"Meriam is Sam's wife."

"This is all very strange, you know."

"It depends," I say.

"No, it doesn't," Christine raises her voice. "Don't you think it's odd living there? Meriam acts as if she delivered you to this universe and nourished you ever since. Sameer this and Sameer that." She tries to imitate Meriam's soft voice.

The bedroom turns into a battlefield. I start thinking how I can get out the door with the least delay. If I move out of the bed, she'll think it's anger. If I leave, I'll hear her shouting after me, "After inviting you to dinner, all you really want is…" Fears I used to have of going to bed with Christine and not being able to leave her afterwards resurge. Affection is there, but not flowing, it's arid as tapping a dry maple tree. I dress slowly and say I have a long day of work tomorrow.

"What shall I tell your friend Riyad when he calls again?" she asks directly.

"Give him my address at Sam's," I say remembering Sam wants to meet some Arabs.

I walk to my car. It's spring. The trees are in full bloom.

What a shame to tread over old lovers like flower petals under a tree.

I seek a buffer zone between Christine and returning to Sam and Meriam. I head towards my Jehovah's Witness friend at Dunkin' Donuts. She is not there. The buffer turns to sadness, a nostalgic sadness. I felt compelled to leave Christine, but now guilt seeps in.

Riyad, my childhood friend, warned me against our marriage. He told me, "No one will understand you like one of your own." Now, six years later, I am embarrassed to meet him, avoiding "I told you so." His studies at Brown keep him out of my range. When we were teenagers, Riyad and I fought against the idea that parents chose the bride. I wanted something outside that. And when I came to the U.S., I loved the independence and spirit of American women. Riyad has changed but I haven't. My family is far away, no danger of an arranged marriage. No relatives with a list of eligible daughters.

But, tearing off my attachment to Christine makes me hold on to my roots in Nazareth. Whenever sadness clouds my head, I feel nostalgic for my hometown.

In Nazareth, Riyad and I were inseparable. Our families are entwined in the history of the town like two grape vines. My life in Nazareth seems so sensible, while the present is filled with bubbling geysers, nonsequiturs.

My marriage now seems even more out of place than the marriage of Riyad's uncle, the last wedding I attended in Nazareth. A sixty-year-old widower marrying a twenty-five-year-old girl, a spinster in Nazareth terms.

Oh, the weddings of Nazareth! Music, Arak, women, belly dancers and friends. We wouldn't miss a wedding, certainly not his uncle's.

The sound of Arabic music, lute and durbakke drum filled the whole neighborhood. Suppressed joy and anticipation in my throat. Music, Arak, belly dancing and friends. I was going to have a great time, even if his uncle was going to devour a young maiden. The Nazarenes appreciated what a young woman could do for an old man. Sex and desire on the lips and minds of everybody. The orgy of feasting, mounting the climax to the end of virginity. Lovers look at one another, women eye each other. Married men stare at the bride. I'm sitting with Riyad and three others. At eighteen, we are eligible bachelors already and sitting at a prominent table. Riyad drinks more than ever before.

"Sameer, are you aware history is being made tonight?"

"What history?" I ask him, one hand holding a stuffed grape leaf, a glass of cloudy Arak in the other.

"Life history," he says.

"Mmmm," I mutter, the atmosphere holding me in its spell.

"It's his wife's life that concerns me," Riyad says. "She'll be a widow in her thirties. Her kids will be fatherless before their teens." A morbid but accurate prediction at the time.

"Nobody seems to be aware of it," I say. Nobody but Riyad seems concerned with the bride's fate. The ritual is at its height. No one in his right mind interrupts an intense social feast. In those moments, individual destinies are obliterated and a mystical spirit hangs in the air. You touch fingers with the real core of life, but it's the last thing you really want to hold.

The festivity is spread out on the roof of a large house which serves as a balcony. The place is milling with people and excitement. Women— old, young, all types—hover over our heads, serving guests, and serving men in particular. Small plates with goat cheese, hummus, tahini, shish-kabob, and fresh Arabic bread. Not pita or any other so-called "pocket" bread, but bread so fresh you want to hold it in your hands and keep smelling its freshness.

Nazarene women are asked to dance. At first they refuse—and only after insistence do they agree. But once they accept, they forget all their resistance and stand to perform their singular body song. Exquisite—the dialogue of Adam and Eve reenacted and renewed.

Nazarenes have a special word for the ecstasy they get at the height of spiritual and physical pleasure. They call it Kaif. By midnight Kaif seeps into the veins. Everybody feels it. The festivity tries to keep this state of Kaif for as long as possible. Each has his own technique, trying to savor it for its last sensation. I shut off and conserve the good feeling until its dissipation. Some get drunk, some get melancholic. In these moments, Nazarenes love to renew their human bonds. They promise each other continued love, friendship and loyalty. They utter their own prayers, wishes, and dreams secretly to themselves—like at New Year— or until a new <u>Kaif</u> prevails. For you know that once you reach <u>Kaif</u>, you can only go down.

By the time Riyad and I leave the wedding it is early morning and we are gracelessly drunk. We stagger down the hill. We end up by Saint Mary's Well. We stop at the well daily in Nazareth because the Virgin Mary was one of its most famous customers, and its water is cool in the summer. Arak is assumed to create the same spell. When Nazarenes emigrate they take a bottle of St. Mary's water with them and attribute many healing miracles to it.

We have a habit that whenever we pass the well at night, we stop and drink from its water and look at the Hannyed wall. You press your Hannyed hand on the wall and make a wish to Saint Mary. All Nazarenes do, Moslems as well as Christians. Nazarene saints served us all indiscriminately. We get that cool sensation only at night, certainly not during the day with groups of tourists hanging over our necks. Saints don't reside where tourist buses stop. Pilgrims should make the last stretch on foot.

Sadness makes me nostalgic. And nostalgia is the Nazareth I know, of my family, of Riyad and other friends. Trying to break loose from my attachment is harder than uprooting an olive tree. I only hurt my own back. Can anything good come out of Nazareth?

I return to Newton. Meriam is alone. Sensing a strange mood, she asks me if I had a good evening.

"It hurts to walk out on Christine—even after divorce," I say. "It's like burying a part of me."

"Sit down, Sameer," she says pointing next to her on the couch. It's the first time I sit by Meriam instead of facing her. She looks into my eyes. "Sameer, are you trying to bury your love for Christine or keep it alive?"

"Tonight all loves seem resurrected," I say.

"Dead relationships should be buried for good," Meriam says with determination.

A vision of a Moslem graveyard I used to pass in Nazareth spreads out in my mind. Gravestones engraved with poetry, of honest lives, pious lives, modest lives, tender parents. Then another vision of an American graveyard with vast meadows of anonymous crosses.

"I never was in a Jewish cemetery," I say unintentionally.

"It's much better to be alive here," Meriam replies with a chuckle.

She is close to me, her face radiating acceptance. Meriam is private, but feeling comfortable. I ask her, "Did you ever live through anything like my relationship with Christine?"

"Wounds heal with time," she says.

"Nature is ruthless," I say. Through the window, I see trees that lost their leaves last fall waiting to bud again in full rapture. Past loves are hard to bury.

"Sameer…dear Sameer," and with great ease Meriam takes my hand in both of hers. "You have lots of sorrow. Why add guilt?"

Meriam holds my hand for a second longer. A strange shiver goes through both of us. She suddenly apologizes. She says, she's tired, she stands. I stand out of politeness. In a sudden move, she puts her arms around me and hugs me. "Good night," she says.

"Good night, Meriam."

CHAPTER 10

Pleasure springs within and washes the world with daylight. It kicks vigor, music, and work into life, and life becomes joyous.

Early the next morning, Meriam cheerfully announces in the presence of Sam, "Sameer, I bet you haven't seen the new Monet exhibit. And there is a poetry reading in Cambridge. You should join us tonight." Meriam weaves a hundred golden strings around our days.

Meriam and I go to Walden Pond for a walk, she's reading Thoreau. We go for a picnic. Sam, noticing the time we spend together, says, "I hope Sameer won't charge me for the escort."

I feel the delicious guilt of a priest catching himself looking at a woman in public.

"Actually you're the most celibate resident we've ever had. Esther was just the opposite."

I drive Meriam to an Arabic grocery store and show her the sweets first, a freshly baked, round tray of baklava. "You should see an Arabic wedding, the sweets, the Jordan almonds wrapped as colorful gifts from the bride, Lekum candy served with coffee, the durbakee drum and Arab women swaying to the music - - hips, breasts and gracious heads."

I take a loaf of Arabic bread. "You should feel it with your fingers— it has to be soft, it has to open. You fill it with homemade jams, apricot, or mulberry, or with omelet and fresh mint—or with tahini and crisp romaine lettuce." I move to the rice in large sacks. "Rice has to be done so there are nice, single grains. What a sprinkle of allspice, nutmeg and cinnamon can do for rice—or a touch of saffron if it's served with fish. Lentils are green, orange, or brown." I remember the warmth of lentil dishes on a cool evening. In front of a rack of spices, I sniff the cinnamon, the nutmeg, the allspice. "They have to blend, a touch of lemon can do wonders on sautéed meat with a clove of garlic."

Meriam looks at me. Then brushing me affectionately, she whispers, "You're not showing me a grocery store, Sameer. You're showing me your past, and I love it."

On Mother's Day, Sam puts his arm around Meriam and announces, "I am declaring Step-Mother's Day! I'm updating the occasion. We have more step-mothers than mothers anyhow. We are taking Meriam out."

I have nothing to do with step-mothers, but they both insist. We walk out together. Meriam pulls Sam to her side and, with ease, draws me to her other side. I have become part of a very delicate balance.

As we walk out, Sam asks, "How about your Palestinian friends? I want to meet Riyad. You said Riyad's an activist. I never met a PLO member before."

I know Riyad is trying to get hold of me. I like my living arrangement, but I am not ready to walk out in the daylight.

It's Mother's Day. In Nazareth, Mother is there everyday. Mother waiting up until I return, to warm my food. Mother spending the whole day selecting fresh green squash, then scraping their surface, hollowing them out, filling them with rice and lamb, and stacking them neatly in the pot. Mother waiting at night until my energy is spent with friends, returning home hungry and happy, Mother there waiting. Mother saying good-bye to me in the morning, loading me with wishes for good luck, wishes against the evil eye. Raise your head my son, she would say. Father's love imparts a thousand horses of strength and confidence. Mother. Mother's love swept away like debris in all directions of the world. Families split, refugees. Israel is built on the remnants of Palestine. The wreckage is scattered. And I am in Newton, Massachusetts.

It's beautiful to see American mothers on Mother's Day with new hairdos and festive dresses, sitting at the heads of tables in restaurants. Sometimes I see sons and their wives, not used to talking with parents, smoking nervously and drinking out of tension. Parents and children drift apart while still in the same country. Try to make sense out of that, out of life.

I live within my head and in a limited social space. Meriam moves in society and she wants me to join her. Hadassah was only the beginning. Jews are curious about their own reflections in the eyes of Arabs. They like my talks, and I slowly learn how to coat my bitter messages. I am invited to many meetings.

Today's meeting is a study group at Temple Sinai. When the session is over, Meriam disentangles me from questioners and we go to the Magic Pan in Boston. We always order praline crepes, a blending of flavors that only the French master.

"Aren't you tired of listening to my politics?" I ask her, testing.

"No, Sameer, I like your point of view. I find myself in disagreement with Sam."

"And how do you and Sam manage political disagreement?"

"Sam, as you know, keeps his serious thoughts to himself," she says, laughing. "He's planning revenge. This morning he said I need to hear the Jewish point of view." Meriam pauses, sips her coffee and adds, "He's inviting us, you and me, to attend a presentation on the Holocaust. The Jews remember the Holocaust every year."

The Jews like to keep their hands in their wounds. I want to ask Meriam if I can speak of Palestinian Holocaust. About pregnant women and children stabbed to death in Deir-Yassin, or shot against olive trees in Kafr-Qasim, about houses demolished and villages leveled while the owners were held watching. But I am in the Magic Pan in Boston, where brass chandeliers hang cozily over tables and luscious plants fall down brick walls. I do not give a vehement response. Affluence dilutes tragedy. Happiness is the best detergent for memory.

I surprise myself saying to Meriam, "I wish there was a world without end."

"Oh, Sameer," Meriam says, "That's a very romantic wish."

"I like the part about the world without end in the prayer," I say. "Glory to the Father and to the Son and to the Holy Spirit. As it was in the beginning, is now and ever shall be, world without end. Amen.

Amen." I like the Magic Pan without end. I want now without end.

"The sacred and the secular?" Meriam asks smiling.

"Grabbing either side is gluttony," I laugh.

Later I try to get out of the Holocaust, but Sam insists and the three of us go. Holocaust descriptions splash an ocean of nightmares, a Vesuvius of blood, panic, and terror. Hannah Arendt had steel moral fiber when, despite the Holocaust, she still insisted that Israelis killing one Arab is equally immoral.

As if Sam wants to lace the experience with his own tonic, he gives me a copy of <u>One Generation After</u>, a magazine for the children of people who survived the Holocaust. Sam put me on their mailing list—and acts on the border of human comedy and tragedy. Sam has the final say.

Between the Oasis and my life with Sam and Meriam, I am caught on two different planets. At the Oasis, there is no leisure. Customers come and go, orders fly around me. I'm becoming professional. I introduce a few Palestinian dishes. Sam wants to give them fancy names with Oasis metaphors, but I insist on keeping their real names. "Kibbee cannot be called 'Oasis Treat' for God's sake," I tell Sam.

Whenever I have a chance, I watch customers. Sam is right. People are at their best when they eat a good meal. Married couples interact mostly with their plates. Dating couples remain attentive. Seeing married partners gaze into the huge space between them, I feel relieved about my lost marriage. Single people come to eat and to talk to anybody, waiters or other customers.

I start recognizing special customers who always demand a different table than the one offered by our hostess. And there are customers who are conscious of eating in public places, who wipe their mouths politely after every bite. Teenagers come walking erect, fresh and resilient, while middle-aged men burdened by experience bend over their tummies. I like our customers. They like our food and enjoy it. The only ones I don't like are those who invariable complain. "Bitching as a lifestyle,"

Sam grins.

In the morning, before the waitresses come, I sit with Sam and plan the menus and supplies for the next day.

The morning following the Holocaust program, I ask Sam something I did not dare ask Meriam. "Why do the Jews keep scratching their own wounds?"

Sam looks at me, surprised. "Two thousand years of fear."

"But why in the U.S.?" I ask. "I can give you statistics on high numbers of Jews in top professions. A Korean friend, a graduate of Harvard, once said, 'The WASPS are very generous. They established Harvard and donated it to the Jews.'"

Evasively, Sam quips, "I thought we only had to put up with the Arabs."

I persist, "I mean, why saturate life with tragedy?"

"But tragedy is part of our life." In unusual seriousness Sam asks, "And what do you suggest? What is your alternative?"

"Open Israel for both Palestinians and Jews. Not a Jewish State but a secular one," I answer.

"There crumbles the dream of David," Sam retorts.

"The Jews dreamed for 2,000 years. What if Palestinians keep their dream of lost land alive two thousand years more?" I ask. The wrath of a destructive dream is devastating.

"Listen, Sameer, ours is not just a dream, it's a battle for survival."

"I've heard that before. It's not survival, but survival of the fittest, I suppose."

"So far so good," Sam says smiling with his fingers crossed. Driving home, Sam suddenly asks me, "Why do we get along so well?"

"It's a wonder." I shake my head.

"Meriam is already a convert," he laughs.

"Truth, of course, overrides," I say, teasing.

"Meriam is fond of you."

44

"Meriam is great."

"Before you moved in with us she was very restless. At one point I thought I was going to lose her."

"I didn't know that."

"I'm still afraid sometimes." Sam never discussed his feelings before. "I don't know if you've noticed, but I have a roving eye. That's how women put it." He looks serious.

"I didn't notice," I answer surprised.

"Meriam is very precious to me, but I still find myself needing other women."

I sit immobile. This revelation, this confidence, comes as a burden, a spiritual chain. Imprisoned in friendship. How should I act to Meriam after this?

"Frankly," I say, hating the fact that I am using that word, "I think Meriam is a treasure." I think to myself, this is a platitude, but I am unable to be specific. "Does Meriam know about these women?"

"Meriam operates ten levels beyond me."

"You're making it difficult for me."

"I know," Sam says with a wicked smile.

Roving eye. The king of the forest hunting for prey, confident his home is warm. Why seduce temple maidens when you have a goddess? Admiration, adulation, sex. When wild mallards couple with tame white ducks in the north, they die with the first snow rather than migrate south and abandon their partners. Shakespeare is right. Nothing is really right or wrong, thinking makes it so. Maybe only a touch of the divine can explain this. But what if the divine is a wicked fisherman, and we are all on the hook under the illusion of a free ride?

"Sam," I burst out, "those women, what do you find in them?" I sound so naive and dogmatic to myself, so innocently ignorant. I try to change my question. "I mean, when you're with Meriam, you're so loving and attentive. Is it an act? Are you playing a different role in every situation?"

"Sameer," Sam says, clearly exasperated, "you want to ask me if I am a fake at home, in the restaurant, with friends, and mistresses?" Sam pauses. "You're pushing me to be serious—you have quite a knack for that."

"Yes, I do, I guess."

"It's true, in the U.S. people are trained to have many faces," Sam continues, "but I wasn't born here. With me it's a different story. For me, God died a long time ago, maybe in Bergen Belsen." And with a violent gesture he slams his cup on the saucer and shatters it into pieces. "For you, God should've died in 1948 when you people were kicked out of Palestine. But if you still hold onto Him, then you are a divine sucker," Sam snaps bitterly.

"I hate to sound like a novice monk, but what do you believe in anyhow? That is, if you believe in anything at all."

"How much time do we have?" Sam asks.

Time is obviously against me. It's 8:00 A.M. Waitresses will be barging in within five minutes.

"You can be my biographer," he says, a sinister smile on his face. "Wouldn't that be fun, a biography of a Zionist by a Palestinian?"

"You owe me an answer," I say, feeling that Sam eluded me one second after the catch.

The morning passes, I am totally absorbed. Sam leaves the Oasis and I am in charge. Between waitresses and customers and the grill, I am covered by the trivial routine of a day in the restaurant. It always happens this way. The day-to-day pressure goes on forever, then suddenly old age. What a terrifying thought, what a terrifying waste.

An old customer, who's become a friend of mine at the Oasis, once revealed that he is going through psychoanalysis at seventy-two.

"What for?" I asked.

"To make sense of my past."

"What for?" I persisted.

"To make sense of the future," he replied.

"What future? Where?"

"Here," he said, pointing to his head. "I don't want to lie in the casket with a foggy head," he said smiling with resignation.

I wish I believed it makes a difference.

I carry Sam's secret like a pregnant woman, overdue for delivery. I arrive in Newton, try to avoid Meriam, walk quickly up to my room.

Meriam calls from downstairs. "You have a special delivery letter."

I go down to get it and exchange quick smiles with her.

"Is anything the matter?" she asks.

"Oh, no," I answer. I take the letter and go upstairs to read it. A letter from Mother. My father is very ill.

The fear that Father is dying hits like a summer storm. I am terrified by its potential lightning. Thinking of Mother left alone, of her pain, of Mother clothed completely in black as the custom dictates, frightens me. My Hippie Christ hanging on the wall—always sensitive to my moods— looks at me with deep melancholy. By the time a letter covers thousands of miles, it snowballs with premonition. What if Father is already dead? The tears of loss grip me. I bury my head in the pillow and sob with my body, my soul, with my past, my present, and mostly with my future. "Oh, no," I cry out loud.

Meriam, alarmed, rushes to the room. "Sameer, for God's sake, what's wrong?"

"My Father had a serious heart attack," I answer, and that is the end of my control. The rest is difficult to grasp or understand.

Meriam lies by me on the bed, hugs me, soothes me, "Sameer, Sameer." Meriam kissing me gently on the cheeks, her arms around me with total acceptance. Then Meriam breaks down crying.

"Oh, Meriam, please don't," I turn to calm her, brush the hair from her eyes. Gently she draws my lips to hers. Meriam kisses me with all the comforting love of a woman, with her lips, and all of her body. I lie in her arms for a long, long time.

What I had feared becomes reality the following morning. A cable arrives at 5:20 a.m. announcing with utmost simplicity, "Father passed away. We love you. Mother."

I phone Mother immediately to comfort her, and I learn through her sobs that Father actually died two weeks before and my family decided to protect me from the painful news and the need to return.

I select a picture of my father and put it on my desk. I light a candle, and pray, not really a prayer. I just talk to him, this time my tears flowing quietly. The candle is small. It burns fast and drips on my table. Father does not respond.

The next day, and the next and the next, I carry my father with me. He is warm and charming. Father telling me, "I believe in you, Sameer, if you believe in what you do." Father coming to visit me in an Israeli jail packed with young Arabs striking for equal pay. Father keeping a smile of confidence on his face. I felt the depth of pain he was concealing. Sitting in the shade of a mulberry tree, Father asking me to read a novel to him when I was eight years old and still stumbling over words, while he's listening with patience to a text read without comprehension. Father.

I start seeing signs of funeral homes I never noticed, elderly women watering geraniums in graveyards. Gravestones that looked cold suddenly seethe with blood and tears. I think of Nazareth where there are no funeral homes, where elderly women are the last to handle the living, the dead. Where people are born at home and, when they die, are carried out in caskets through the front door. Where there is always one last desperate attempt by the widow and children to keep the casket at home, then from being carried out of the church. Where the scream "no" to the pallbearers with all the intensity of love and the horror of death.

I start noticing funeral processions and relatives enclosed in brightly lit cars. In the city, grief only interrupts traffic.

It's late July and we are sitting in the garden by red geraniums and white daisies. Sam, aware of my pain, suggests a vacation.

I am not enthusiastic about Sam's idea. "Where you arrive does not matter so much. It's what sort of person you are when you arrive," I say smiling. "I credit Seneca with the thought."

"It's better if you stay with us, Sameer." Meriam looks away.

"Can we help in any way? It's a dirty deal," Sam says shaking his head. "Ashes to ashes."

The cliché about death suddenly resonates with chilling truth.

"What did your father do?" Sam asks me.

"He enjoyed living," I answer. I will always remember Father's delight in simple pleasures. Father arranging a basket of fruit or a bouquet of flowers.

"I'm sure he died a happy man," Sam says, "happier than most fathers I know."

Meriam looks at Sam, questioning.

"I bet your father received a lot of love in return," Sam says, the flash of a troubled look on his face. Then he adds, "In the U.S., being a father is a one-way street."

Dead-end street, I think to myself.

"Sam is upset," Meriam explains. "Esther skipped Father's Day without calling."

"Fathers are the ones who give all the time—give, give, give. If I get a birthday card, I become suspicious. What do they want this time?" Sam blurts out. "Here, parents operate like N.A.S.A. We only have kids to launch them."

Anger curdles humor, like sour milk.

"Don't believe him," Meriam says. "He loves them a lot."

"This probably sounds sacrilegious, Sameer, I never really wanted to be a father. Their mothers talked me into it, a tie between us they claimed. But, of course, I love my children, that's why it hurts. When they're around, I still need three martinis before I can relax," Sam smiles nervously. "And about seven martinis before I can see their mothers! There should be service duty—like the army—thou shall honor your father for two years. Stay at home and talk to him." And after a pause, "You still have to meet my kids. I still have to break the news to them."

"What news?" Meriam asks.

"Well, that Sameer is a Palestinian."

"Oh, Sam, really," Meriam says.

"A budding rabbi for a son and a fanatic Zionist for a daughter," Sam exclaims.

I never expressed a wish to meet them. Although curious, I sit puzzled by the exchange.

"You must have beautiful memories of your father," Meriam says, saving Sam the consequences of his impromptu confessions.

"It must hurt to see how blind life is to your sadness," Sam tells me. "Jews don't shave for seven days after a death in the family. The Irish drink for seven. It's just a question of priority," he says with forced cheer.

"In Nazareth we wear black bands on our sleeves," I say. I carry my black band inside me.

"I don't know what it is, but here life drives a wedge between fathers and sons." Sam suddenly looks very far away.

Meriam closes her eyes against the morning sun.

In Arab villages people spread mats outside and spend long evenings together. Fathers, sons, relatives sitting, talking or just silent. Sons get blessings from their fathers. "May Allah assist you." "May Allah keep you healthy." They give these blessings at every move. And sons do follow in their father's footsteps. Will this last in Nazareth? But what lasts? Our Father who art in Heaven.

Death jams my living. I try to escape its jolt, but it echoes from long distance. I overwork, but when the day is over the memory of Father seeps in to fill my room. The summer rushes past. A piece of me is back home. In Nazareth, August is a month of short shadows, the sun blazing mostly on top of your head. People rest for endless hours on their shaded verandas or under grape vines. Stillness and heat create thirst. The Ibreeque is nearby, a pottery jar the Nazarenes have used to chill drinking water since biblical days.

In August you can smell dryness. Nature sweats and dries in heat like ebony. We wake up earlier than usual, "with the dew," Father used to say. It's the best time to pick fruits from our garden - - prickly pears, figs, and grapes. And sometimes we stay awake long after dusk whispering as darkness spreads. The sky looks so close, the stars are always there. One by one, we bid Father and Mother goodnight, "May you wake up to a good morning," and then we sleep soundly. We love staying around the elders, relatives, friends - - resting within their protective zone. Time is sipped slowly from aromatic coffee cups filled and refilled. Mother roasts white pumpkin seeds, or dark watermelon seeds, and there are pistachios and salted garbanzo beans. Life unfolds slowly and with natural ease.

Until the jolt of history cracked the ceiling. Israel was forced upon us in war. Palestinian towns emptied from fear. Jaffa, Haifa, Safad, Tiberias, Jerusalem. Nazareth fell with no resistance. Land confiscated, people fled. For the first time we were left shaking in front of foreign mirrors. When the beautiful past is shattered, it becomes a legend - - and acquires the strength of a supernatural myth. All of it, the parents in it, the soil, the events.

I have changed from a teacher to a hired cook, orbiting between Newton Center, the Oasis and my night classes.

My life has crossed Sam's, we spark with surprises. My face glows with memories of warm childhood, his face burns with memories of unreturned love from his children. Still we understand each other. And Meriam sits to the side holding both of us closer. Eve.

CHAPTER 11

My feelings reach a log-jam. I do need to get away, take a vacation, step outside myself, go to a place where I'll be totally lost, where I won't know the language. I look at a map. Quebec looks close yet French is foreign to me. I decide to drive north on a vacation to nowhere.

I look at my Hippie Christ. "You went to the wilderness outside Nazareth to search for yourself. My wilderness will be the Gaspe Peninsula," I say with irony. Sameer will take Sameer out, and I'll take my own Father with me. I'll conduct my personal funeral, spread his memories on the shores of the St. Lawrence. I'll drive around the Gaspe. I need to go to another planet.

On the morning of my departure, Meriam leaves me a basket of fruits and The Little Prince. Sam leaves me a bottle of Arak. "Holy water, you may need," he writes on the label.

I drive crossing New Hampshire, then Maine. All is green. Nazareth is brown now, the earth gushes waves of heat like a sauna. Another hundred miles and I find myself on the shores of St. Lawrence. "What now?" I cry. Then slowly I notice the landscape, churches on hilltops and eel traps on the shore. Churches with gray aluminum steeples towering over life, over the graves of their builders. Churches overlooking the river, and overlooking eel traps. Eel traps looking like the original sin, unavoidable. Bread and pies sold along highways from houses splashed with bright colors of red, white and shades of green. I pass a motel called "Oasis" in St. Jolie. I take its picture. In Quebec, I shift between memories of Father and moments of joy.

I come across a festival on the banks of a river. People are waiting for returning fishermen. There will be prizes for the largest fish. They're waiting with their glittering knives. The river does not disappoint. Boats return in order of the largest catch. Fishermen with bloodshot eyes hold up large sturgeon. The slaughter is still the climax of the ritual. They drink, fillet, barbecue and eat.

I take my bottle of Arak, sit at a picnic table and join the drinking crowd. Girls, watching boys, watching cars, the weightless look of youth everywhere. Youth driving fast in and out. Dolphins splashing in the fury of their sperms. An old couple joins me at the table. The old man faces his wife. I notice her refined bony forehead marked with grace and old age. They look at each other, share small gestures of affection, and an apple. Acceptance is more durable than love. Their warmth touches me.

Dizzy with Arak, I rub my cheeks with cold water and continue driving. All along the river people sit facing the highway. People who built a dream house by the river sit facing the road—not the wide river. Observing the human smile of a passerby is warmer than staring at eternity.

I open <u>The Little Prince</u>. If only I could observe the world like St. Exupery, from the distance of a pilot. Only from the sky could St. Exupery see his little prince-on another planet, carefully watering a simple flower he loves.

Venus always glitters bright above Nazareth. I heard her in the chants of convents near my home. I wrote her love letters since I was eleven. I watched her from a distance on the seven mountains surrounding Nazareth. She was always there, looking with compassion on a town burdened with its history, eaten by political malice, holier than thou with its unholiness. I have known her all my life. She is the mother who nurtures her seven children in the absence of a father.

In Nazareth love is a forbidden fruit. Lines of Sufi poetry ring in my memory: "God, you created beauty to tempt us, and ordered us to abstain. You are beautiful and you love beauty. Why shouldn't your worshippers - - like you - - be allowed to love beauty?"

After two weeks I cross the border back to Massachusetts. I feel I understand my Hippie Christ more than before. I'll tell him, "You loved the wrong people. The forbidden fruit." I hear Sam intrude on my thoughts, "Christ never belonged to your town, an illegitimate child never belongs. If they had accepted Christ, the course of history would have been changed." Pain generates religious history. The thought alarms me, and Nazareth still doesn't see beyond the boundaries of its own sunrise and sunset.

It feels good to be back. The Hippie Christ looks at me accusingly, so I tell him, "You fell in love with Mary Magdalene after your wandering in the wilderness. Don't deny it."

I leave my suitcase on the floor and open a letter from Mother. She is worried about me - - worried that grief will affect my health, will deprive me of daily happiness. Mothers and saints.

CHAPTER 12

I open a letter from Riyad. The letter is half consolation for the death of my father and half reprieve for disappearing after my divorce.

Sam, realizing I'm home, calls me downstairs to join them for supper. Face to face with Meriam. Sweet flavors of food arrive from the kitchen. Cinnamon dough, butter and sugar. Woman fed this to man as long as she nursed him. There is a sense of reunion around the table. I talk about my trip.

"Is solitude the answer to grief?" Meriam asks.

"Life is the only answer."

"I like that," Sam interrupts, his mouth full, "life is the best answer."

I continue, "But you know, somehow the moral order gets shattered with death."

"Good," Sam says. "Moral orders bore me. People end up doing the things they want anyway."

We laugh, each one of us for a different reason.

"Sam, the master pragmatist." Meriam shakes her head.

"Survivor," he corrects her.

"Did you write about your feelings while in Gaspe?" Meriam asks.

"No, I couldn't make sense of anything."

"Don't worry, Sameer. It will come back. You must translate every feeling into the truest sentence you have ever written." She touches my passions with ease.

"Smith College was not wasted," Sam announces.

"Smith plus Hemingway," Meriam answers, ruffling his hair.

"Plus your father," Sam adds.

"Oh, talking about my father…" Sam and Meriam look at each other knowingly.

"No, you break the news," Sam grins.

"What news?" I inquire with caution.

"Oh, nothing bad," Meriam laughs. "You're invited to visit my parents in Westport, Connecticut. It will be good for you."

"I'm surprised your parents even know I exist."

"Sam 'begged off,' his own words," Meriam smiles affectionately at him.

"In-laws should be visited only under duress," Sam responds laughing. "But you really should accept the invitation. The Oasis is closed, it's a holiday weekend anyway."

I must look puzzled, for Meriam quickly adds, "They're curious about you."

I get wary whenever I hear of curiosity about me. I've learned the hard way to keep my ego within the confines of a very modest rug. It hurts less. But Meriam's parents do excite my own curiosity.

"That will be nice," I say, counting ten days until that weekend.

"Great," Meriam says sounding satisfied.

I wonder if it would be proper to go without Sam. Meriam certainly knows what is proper, I reassure myself.

"You're back from Canada just in time. Another week and I would've lost my customers, and my waitresses." To the tune of "You are my sunshine, my only sunshine," Sam sings, "I have my chef back, my Kosher chef back."

"That's why you'll never make it in business," Sam snaps.

"Don't listen to him," Meriam tells me, obviously happy. "Sameer is going to be a writer!"

"Sameer will earn more money at the Oasis than he ever will as a writer," Sam declares.

Going back to work and classes blots out my consciousness. Sam's worry about his customers is well founded. My assistant at the Oasis was using a bit of his East European flair on my Arabic recipes and the results were devastating. "A Salvation Army kitchen," one customer tells me. My writing class piles up assignments and papers. My thoughts are milling with excitement, with life.

The ramblings of life do not allow wakes to go on forever.

CHAPTER 13

The morning of departure Sam insists on fixing us breakfast.

"If people stop eating, I'll go bankrupt," he says.

Meriam has her hair pulled back. Beautiful profile with a Nefertiti neck. Two pieces of handcrafted silver glittering on her ears. Dressed expensively casual, in a turquoise Shetland sweater over elegantly white jeans. I feel a touch of excitement and pray that my face does not betray me.

Meriam leaves Sam with a kiss on his cheek. "Have fun." Turning to me with a shade of a smile on her face, "Sam is going to have Israeli house-guests."

"I'll feed them Kosher food and they'll fill me up with politics," he says.

"Is that all?" Meriam looks closely at him.

"Yes," Sam is brief. Sam wants us out of the way.

"He gets kind of touchy about his Israeli visitors," Meriam says pulling out of the driveway.

I don't attach any significance to her comment. When I wonder what Sam might do, and my mind can only imagine him in a long orgy. I am happy to be on the way to Westport. The Connecticut countryside is in early fall glory. Blue sky, the first red maple leaves, and we are in a white Continental. I look at Meriam with no restraint.

We pass a wild pheasant, slowing down to look at it. It doesn't act frightened. It's a miracle pheasants survive. We drive through Connecticut back roads, nestled wealth in huge estates. Along the way, homes are decorated early for Halloween—stuffed and strangled effigies, witches and nightmares hanging over roofs, and sitting in yards. Nightmares take shape in front yards. I have many questions for Meriam about herself and Sam and me, but I don't ask.

We stop at an herb farm for lunch. The salad is a bed of flowers. The main dish is lamb. The place is filled with dry herbs hanging from the ceiling, with wealthy single women, and many New England families. The visitors listen in awe to a woman with a huge amber necklace talking about herbs and mint, and how mint garlands were worn by philosophers in Greece. It's amusing how gullible American wealth is to the primitive and rustic. In Nazareth, we say mint is a rude plant, it survives all seasons and it multiplies.

The Connecticut garden has an olive tree with fresh silver leaves. It reminds me of the orchards of olive trees in the Galilee, valleys of tranquility. Trees age with expressive trunks, like faces of old men, roots older than generations of men, and branches with cool shade where farmers rest in hot summers.

"Generations of Arab farmers planted olive trees for their grandsons," I say to Meriam. Meriam engulfs me with attentiveness.

We leave the farm and drive south. A picnic with Meriam is a picnic with Renoir. A picnic with Monet. Am I the last of the Romantics? Every lover is. Watching a woman you love is like watching the surface of an ocean, it engages all the senses.

Back in the car, I say, "I can't believe that I'm spending a weekend with you."

"Neither can I. Sam doesn't mind."

"I cherish my friendship with both of you."

"We owe you much more than you owe us." Noticing my surprise, Meriam adds, "You've added a lot to us. You're the dearest friend I have. There are many things you need to know about us. We never seem to have enough time together. Actually, before you joined us, I was going through a difficult time, disenchantment with love, marriage. Sam and I haven't made love for a long time."

Stunned with the abrupt revelation, no words come to my mouth.

"And this is in strict confidence," Meriam bites her lower lip. "Sam has many affairs with other women. I know and I don't mind it, most of the time," she tries to laugh, but starts to cry. "He doesn't know that I know. Our drives are very remote from each other. And he doesn't want children. Oh, the things I am telling you."

"Please don't stop."

"Before you came to live with us, Sam was running scared, he thought he might lose me. I was depressed. I know how deeply he cares for me." Meriam slows at a stop sign, then continues. "I love his love of life. His vitality. I don't think that he goes with other women because of our lack of sex," she hesitates. "I think that it's as if his needs are never fulfilled, and will never be. I don't think he can help it. I believe he was born in a state of insatiable thirst, and he will die with it. Now I've told you everything."

"Everything?"

"Almost," she says, struggling to control her tears. "Can we pull to the side?" She parks in a rest area. "I shouldn't be crying because I am so happy." Meriam's tears run even faster.

I dry her tears—and hug her.

"Oh Sameer, I love you."

I touch her lips. I tell her I love her, I love her. I caress her passionate body, all of her beautiful body, and for the first time I feel her firm breasts under an almond silk bra. She helps me unfasten her bra and I undress her gently.

We come to each other with the fervor of religious pilgrims, but we trespass over sacred territory all the way to the alter. Then, like all lovers, we sit and recount all the moments we spent together and how we felt, when we fell in love and how early. Meriam's tears wash a path for joy.

"Does Sam know how you feel about me?" I am worried.

With her fingers playful in my hair, she says, "Sameer, my magician, the wonders you bring to my life." She doesn't answer me.

We are only a few miles away from Meriam's parents. "Do you think I'll be able to hide my feelings in front of your parents?"

"Everybody suspected I loved you before you did," Meriam laughs and fixes her makeup.

"Will I be able to conceal my love from your parents?"

"Of course, my love."

"I don't have what you'd call a poker face. Maybe I'll have to move out."

"Absolutely not. We loved each other before. Now we know we do, that's all." She sounds confident.

CHAPTER 14

I like Meriam's mother immediately. She greets us in front of a grand, old house filled with chimneys.

"Meriama, we've been waiting for you. You must be Sameer. You look just like Meriam described you - -handsome. Your dad is in his study."

She takes my arm, a slim woman, shorter than Meriam, and tells me she knows all about me and I should feel at home. I am curious about what she knows. She leads us to her husband. Meriam's father is seated, pipe in hand, in his library surrounded by pictures of Marx and Buber, the Jewish philosopher.

"Sameer, am I pronouncing your name right? Call me Martin," he says standing.

"And I am Vera."

Martin, Vera and Meriam. Meriam hugs her father and stays in his arms for a long time. He grows taller and his eyes brighten.

"I'll show Sameer to his room. Richard will join us for dinner." Vera leads me upstairs.

Fresh flowers are on the table. A picture of Meriam, with two long pigtails arched to the sides of her head, her arm around her brother Richard. Meriam has not talked much about her brother except to warn me, laughing, that "he's a social experience." Books and plants are everywhere. I like the combination of wealth and education. Martin is a professor at The New School. Vera is a pianist.

Vera leaves me to refresh. For some reason I need to look at myself in the mirror. Events are happening so fast. I need assurance it is all real. Life happens first, making sense of it comes later. In the mirror, my face is still there with the pronounced features of my family, my big black eyes are bigger with bewilderment.

I join them in the living room, comfortable black leather couches, and grand piano to the side, busts of Goethe and Bach, art nouveau vases and lamp shades.

Martin plunges me straight into conversation. "What do you think about it, Sameer? We were talking about women before you came. In your experience, comparing Arab, Jewish and American women, when one sorts out cultural differences, is there much left in common? Is there really a universal human nature?" he adds a nervous laugh.

Is he trying to find out how I feel about Meriam in a heavily camouflaged academic net? Can he see it in my eyes already? Why is human nature so elusive to academicians when it is right here sitting in their living room? But I am starting to feel comfortable in intellectual dialogue. It's like mastering a chess game.

I answer with a typical evasion, "Could we really talk about human nature outside culture? Isn't it a cultural concept?"

Suddenly I think of Sam. "If you want to know human nature, come to the Oasis," he'd have said. "I'll show you human nature."

I look at Meriam. She is happy near her father, sitting by his side on the couch.

"Mothers nurture their children with the same devotion everywhere. And children love their parents," I say.

"And how is it between men and women?" Vera asks me, a spark of joyous mischief in her eyes.

"Both Jewish and Arab women are loved by men," I say, and bring a beautiful blush to Meriam's face.

"Religion claims man is born with a certain nature, but I feel man only acquires it with culture," Vera says smiling.

"If that's the case, then shouldn't human nature differ between various cultures?" Martin persists. "Somehow I feel culture is too rigid a tool to explain human nature. We become enslaved by the tools we use." "In Nazareth, we break cheese with our hands, here you use a cheese cutter," I say. "Does the cheese taste the same?" I smile to myself remembering how Arab farmers build an argument. They always ground the discussion in earthy examples. "Working as a cook is spilling into my logic. The ingredients are spilling into my arguments," I laugh.

"The eaters might insist they have different flavors," Martin says. "Is it in the taste buds, or all in the mind?"

"Take music," Vera says, "I once saw a jazz group drive an American audience to great motion and excitement. I saw the same group in Stockholm, and all it brought were gentle, controlled taps from the Swedes who, mind you, were raving about it afterwards. Was their satisfaction the same?"

A loud sports car pulls in the driveway. "Richard finally made it," Martin says.

Richard enters, his eyeglasses in his hand, kisses his mother, then Meriam.

"Mimi, you always make me drive home in rush hour, took me half an hour to cross the bridge downtown!" Turning to me, "What do you find in her anyhow?"

"You have to get used to Richard's brand of politeness," Meriam explains to me.

"I had a horrible day," Richard continues uninterrupted. "My secretary," he waves his hand, "is having all kinds of marital problems. I don't know why she got married in the first place. So I ended up typing my own report, and John kept calling me all day."

"Oh," his father's disapproval shows in spite of himself.

"Well, we're thinking about sharing an apartment," Richard proceeds. "What's for dinner?"

I discover fast that Richard doesn't care if you answer his questions. His mouth moist, his hands soft, there is a touch of decadence about him. I'm on my guard.

"Pork chops," Vera says.

"Great, but isn't he prohibited from eating it?" Richard asks, glancing in my direction.

"So are you, Richard," Meriam says, laughing.

"I love pork," I say.

"I find religious prohibitions archaic," Martin says. "They're as old as dinosaur bones."

"God is the prime dinosaur," Richard interrupts. "Calcified shortly after the act of creation."

"Probably in desperation over what She says," Vera says laughing.

"We're not shocking you, are we?" Richard wiggles his glasses. "You fell into a den of heretics, and former zealots."

"We don't need to get into that right away," Meriam pleads.

"Let's have a drink." Martin goes to fix them. Obviously he's already used to Richard. Parents have no choice.

We carry our drinks to the dining room. A grand room with black chairs that have high, stiff backs. I sit by Meriam, facing Vera and Richard. Martin heads the table.

"I suppose you Arab men are expected to be married by eighteen, have three wives and ten kids by twenty-five," Richard says, not looking me in the eyes.

"We plan to catch up with India," I say and wonder how long it's going to take me to lose my temper.

"Some parents enjoy parenting," Martin says.

"Daddy, we love you too." Meriam pats his hand. Meriam, placed between us, is courting us both.

"How is Sammy?" Richard looks at me fleetingly. "I'm amazed you two are managing together."

"Magnificently," Meriam says.

"If you only knew what Zionist claws you've fallen into," Richard continues.

"Sameer." Martin raises his glass. "This is the right moment to welcome you to us. In this house, all "isms' are suspicious."

"Absolutely," Meriam clicks my glass.

"Thank you, I am very happy to be here. Meriam and Sam have been very kind to me." Why do I invoke Sam's name?

"Sam also wanted us to meet you." Vera serves me first.

"If you ever consider going to school full time, you can always stay with us and go to the New School. Buber is my idol, and he believed there's a place for both Arabs and Jews in Palestine. So do I," Martin adds.

"That is very nice, Dad," Meriam says, happy with the warmth of her parents.

Richard starts digging. "Have you noticed, Sameer, a nice meal always generates pleasant conversation?"

"Should I take this as a compliment for my cuisine?" Vera asks.

"You are impossible, Richard." Meriam doesn't take him too seriously.

"What's missing is a reader," Richard continues, "like at Roman banquets. Someone who will read us poetry or a nice part of a thriller while we're eating dinner."

"Roman Catholics still have them in monasteries," Martin says.

"I'd have a problem listening to what they read there. Maybe we should plug our ears and listen to our own individual music just like joggers."

"People are afraid to be left with themselves," Vera says.

"I think people are more afraid to confront silence," I say.

"Is man really afraid to be left alone now more than before?" Martin asks. "Are we changing for the worse?"

"I really believe in progress," Meriam says. "That men and women improve."

"In the past, people had their ears tuned to all the voices of the night, of nature. Arab farmers still do, and they form their philosophy of life by watching nature."

"In this technological society, Sameer, philosophy is a dirty word," Martin says. "When I say I am a philosophy professor at a cocktail party, the response is like being introduced as a funeral director. People don't know what to say."

"C'est la vie," Vera says.

"C'est la mort," Richard says, laughing.

The meal is delicious. Pork Cazabra, done with wine and pine nuts. A touch of class and a touch of austerity shows in the china, the crystal, even the brand of good coffee that follows, and the Bach that Vera plays on her grand piano. I feel I am on a honeymoon.

Vera suggests a walk to the beach.

Richard declines, "I've got to run. See you tomorrow," and hugs Meriam.

Vera walks with Martin, ahead of us, her arm around him.

"I really love them," Meriam tightens her grip on my arm, "and you," she whispers. "They have been taking these after-dinner walks ever since I remember. It's their time to plan and plot for the next day. They're constantly interested in each other. Father is a mess when it comes to business matters. Mother is the brains there. He says he makes words and she makes coins."

"I remember my first lecture in philosophy, 'The is that does not exist, and the nothingness that does.' How could anybody make money on a statement like that?"

Overhearing us, Martin looks back. "Did Meriam tell you much about our family? I was supposed to become a rabbi. Instead I married a rabbi's daughter."

"That cured him completely," Vera says laughing.

Martin waits for us to catch up with them. "It was a perfectly arranged marriage between two Orthodox families. I tried to convince Meriama of the wisdom of arranged marriage." Martin laughs at the memory. "So one day my daughter comes and announces, 'Father, I love a man who is divorced twice, has two children, is a Zionist, and has no academic degree.'" Over the years, Martin's shock has faded into a broad smile.

"Father," Meriam pleads.

"Arranged marriages are still around," Vera interrupts.

"Instead of the rabbi, the computer and the evening tabloid are the matchmakers. I wouldn't mind matching up Richard, but he has his own lifestyle." She turns to Martin. "I'm not sure I'm happy about Richard moving in with John, I don't think it's a wise step for Richard."

"It doesn't seem that I'll be a grandfather very soon, from either side, Richard or Meriam." Martin is pressing the issue.

"No chance," Meriam says.

"Why?" Vera entreats.

"Sam says there's no certainty in life."

"But you have no financial worries, Meriama," Vera says.

"No, Sam feels the unknowns and traumas of modern life are too much to take, we should not subject a baby to them."

"And here I thought you were happy," Martin says.

"I was never, ever happier," Meriam closes the discussion. I read a lot into her statement.

"It's so beautiful by the ocean," Vera inhales deeply. "Our senses get completely clogged if we don't listen to nature."

"Ver—Raa—Lee." Martin hugs her.

"Have you ever seen a couple this much in love," Meriam is exhilarated.

"We believe in sweeping our differences outdoors, not under the carpet," Martin echoes back.

"I have great memories of walks and runs and empty shells on this beach." Meriam takes off her shoes. The ocean has liberated something in her reserve.

I look at her and a tide of desire floods me. We wade in the water, collect a few shells, and walk back to the house.

Martin's life is highly routinized, I discover. Soon after the walk, he'll retire to his office and Vera will do the same. They do not share offices.

As we enter the house, Meriam says, "We share the bathroom on the third floor. Martin and Vera sleep on the second floor."

I tell Martin, Vera and Meriam goodnight, and take the New Yorker to my room.

About an hour later Meriam opens the bathroom door and finds me brushing my teeth. She is wearing a green nightgown with thin straps, her nude body all beaming under it.

I look at her speechless. All I can do, all I want to do, is be close to her. My senses peak like never before, my lips absorbing every sensation – feeling, touching, and loving. Meriam in my arms, all of her bending toward me, whispering my name. I carry her to bed. Love pours strength and she feels delicate and clinging. We kiss and I sense her excitement.

"Sameer, I love you. Sameer, I want you. Sameer, I want you," she keeps repeating. Her cheeks are wet, her tears are flowing. "I am so happy," she whispers a moment before our total surrender.

We lie in bed. I open my eyes and see features I hadn't seen before: a mark on her left shoulder, another below her breasts. Suddenly I remember that "to know" also means "to make love" in both Arabic and Hebrew.

"I've always loved you, Sameer, since your first visit. Sam teases me, saying the only peaceful Middle East is in our house. Now everything is right with the world."

Towards the early hours of the morning my eyes close, my head happily rests on Miri's breast, and I am carried into a deeper silence. Desire dims my conscience, at least for now.

Next morning, Meriam, not Vera, is serving breakfast. Vera looks restless. She takes me around the house explaining its history, 1829, and the art work in each room. I am afraid she is going to confront me about Meriam. We walk out to the garden.

She turns abruptly. "Martin never accepted Sam. I know Sam is a good man and provided Meriama with a good life. Martin never accepted Sam," she repeats. She seems to sense my surprise, for she adds, "We're very happy, Sameer, she found a friend in you. She has been talking about you ever since you met." Vera looks at me, the eyes of a mother, deep, understanding, and worried. "Please don't hurt her, take good care of her."

Before I can voice my promise, and make a fool of myself, she changes the topic. "Meriam must have told you about Richard."

"No."

"The circumstances of his divorce were a great shock to Martin." I must look perplexed for she rushes to explain, "You see, Richard discovered he didn't need a wife, but a male partner. He was still married when he found out."

"It must have been hard on everybody," I say, relieved I do not have to discuss this with Meriam.

"Martin did not want Richard to be a macho football player, but he certainly did not expect him to be a homosexual. Richard is testing our limits, Sameer. He's bringing his friend to dinner with him tonight. We thought we'd alert you ahead of time." Vera shakes her head in disbelief. "Absolutely incredible."

Meriam and Martin are approaching us in the garden and discussing the same concern, for Martin looks at me and says, "Richard is coming out and I don't know whether to pat myself on the back as a liberal father or condemn myself. Sameer, what do you think?"

Academics get caught in their own theories. I try to avoid being entangled in Martin's deliberations. I'd be treading in very shallow waters. "It's a question of love," I say. "As a father you simply love him." After last night I sound too wise to my taste.

Fortunately Martin overlooks my answer and continues, "I know all the arguments about freedom of choice, live and let live. I'm disgusted with myself because I'm uncovering an old fogey conservative under all of this. I'd simply like to have a grandchild, damn it, one that carries my name. Instead, I end up feeling guilty. My father would have excommunicated me if I acted like Richard." Martin pauses. "He was an Orthodox rabbi."

"Don't blame yourself," Vera reassures her husband. "It's a case of no-fault creation, like a no-fault divorce. The Orthodox have the chutzpah to praise divine will, and then turn around and be critical of its children."

"Your father dreamed of a business career for you and see how you ended up." Meriam puts her arm around her father.

"Did you notice that Richard was unusually snappy yesterday?" Martin asks, then looks at his watch. "It's only 11:00 a.m. What time is dinner?"

"Seven."

"Calm down, Daddy," Meriam tells him. "We love Richard just like Sameer said. And you know he loves you."

Martin pulls up four garden chairs. We sit in a crescent, the view unfolding in front of us—green lawns, maple trees, and the ocean.

Vera brings us espresso, with lemon zest on the side. "Be careful, Martin, your expectations for Richard are getting rigid, a type of trap."

"We're both already trapped." Martin stands up, pounding his pipe on his heel to empty it. "Trapped like in a Chinese iron shoe. This friend of Richard's, would be my son-in-law or daughter-in-law? Even the linguistics are problematic."

"Language is very indiscreet," Vera says.

"Richard is a brilliant lawyer," Meriam adds.

Thank God Meriam has an eye for goodness. "I believe it," I say laughing. "I felt I was on the witness stand yesterday."

"I'm going to drive Sameer around town and along the shore. He's curious about where I grew up."

"I'm not sure it's a match for Nazareth, but it's pretty," Vera says approvingly.

We exit just in time. "I was afraid Martin would start asking me what I am to him, linguistically," I kid Meriam.

"I know what you are to me, Sameer. All I can think about today is last night."

She parks by the ocean and we walk dreamily to the dunes. A kiss of love from Meriam is a gift from Aladdin's lamp. It carries me to a different world. My eyes open to appreciate Meriam's beautiful olive complexion, and my lips feel it. All the distractions fade in the distance, cars, city, the noon sun—and we forget the sticky sand on our naked bodies.

"I never felt like this," Meriam keeps repeating.

Back at the house, Vera tells me I'll be sitting by Martin. Meriam will sit across from us. My consolation is that I'll be facing Meriam, not Richard. It is quite clear that we'll be a buffer zone between Martin and Richard's male friend. The thought doesn't really put me at ease. Buffer zones often become the target.

For dinner Meriam wears a red dress of raw silk that flows seductively over her, an open collar and a dazzling silver necklace. Both Vera and Martin are dressed formally. Martin is wearing a suit, and academic's way of establishing distance. Vera is in a long brown dress. I feel like a chameleon, dressed in the mood of the house.

The house is under the spell of a rite of passage, the first visit of Richard's partner. The absurdity of the guests tonight strikes me—Meriam's adulterous lover and Richard's gay lover; it conjures up wild memories in my mind.

I remember my brother coming with his bride. After the wedding, the first visit is to his parents, the second visit is to the church. My brother enters with Suad, his bride, her parents, and brothers and sisters. There is excitement. First lemonade, freshly squeezed lemons from our garden, made with chilled water and a drop of rose water for flavor. And then pistachios and, in the summer, red melon. The younger brothers and sisters of the bride run out into our garden, climbing fig trees, mulberry trees sampling grapes, pomegranates. They return, their mouths wild with patches of red and blue, their new clothes thoroughly broken in.

Food eases tension better than anything. In Nazareth after the third stuffed eggplant, squash, or grape leaf, you can't help sitting comfortably. You praise the hostess, and then praise Allah for his grace, and then you face the host's hospitality. He insists, "How about another eggplant to please me, and one more to please me." And knaffee, baklava and Arabic coffee. You savor your coffee and sip it, loudly.

I feel like sipping my coffee out loud tonight.

And then the long lingering at the door before departure. An exit is never abrupt. "Please greet your uncle and your cousin," we tell the in-laws. We shake hands goodnight. The bride leaves feeling welcome and comfortable. My brother is proud that everything was just right. Now it's his mother-in-law's turn to invite us, and the turns never stop. Mother tells me later, "I think we were lucky in our choice. Suad is everything we expected her to be."

What if I enter Nazareth with Meriam?

Martin takes me to the side. "I'm not sure I'll be able to stay around after dinner. I hope you'll excuse my retreat."

"Certainly," I assure him.

John enters first carrying a black shoulder bag. Slight, energetic, defiant. "I'm John Medford," he announces.

"What can I offer you?" Martin asks while we're still standing in the front hallway. Weather and drinks are good seawalls and wave breakers. You don't have to face each other's eyes.

Richard steps in. "John is trying to kick the habit. We better not tempt him."

"I could stand a cocktail," John says indignantly.

"No. Soda water and misery for you." Richard never loses his politeness. This time he adds a captivating smile.

Vera comes to greet them. I am sure it's hard on mothers to face their son's partners or intruders—from either sex.

"Vera." John walks to her with familiarity. "We've spoken on the phone. Do I look the way you expected?"

Vera looks at him with stamina and control. In a split second I see all the benevolence a mother can muster. "A million times handsomer."

"How should I take that?" he asks.

"With Mother you always get the benefit of the purest doubt," Richard intervenes. "That's more than one usually deserves."

"Would it bother you if I fix drinks for the rest of us?" Martin asks John. I detect imposed formality.

"I'd call this torture, but it's a free country." John answers. Then he looks at me, a new target. "What do Arabs do in a situation like this?"

"They sit around and cover their drinks with their hats," I say.

"The red Fez covering the forbidden Arak in a café," John says, surprising me.

"Exactly. How do you know that?"

"My father was in the foreign service. Bagdad, Damascus, Cairo."

"Have you been to Nazareth?"

"Have I been there? Lost my camera in the Church of Annunciation—but had the most wonderful time. We were invited to dinner by one of the notables. Two wives, large house, marble columns. Blonde people if you can believe it. But no women sat with us, except my mother. She loved the attention she got from the men."

"It's always amusing what people think about your hometown," I say, trying to side-step his comments.

"Nazareth is…," Richard starts.

Meriam interrupts him, "Sameer is sensitive about his hometown."

"The first time I was there," Richard continues, "I had diarrhea, the second time I bought a bunch of crosses made from an olive tree. I didn't know what to do with them."

"People with weak stomachs should never go there," I respond.

Vera leads us to the dining room, just in time. I'm edgy about the role I'm playing, a scapegoat for tensions between Meriam's brother and his lover.

"Richard tells me you're a journalist," Martin says politely to John.

"Trying to become one," John replies. "Not yet discovered."

Vera bends attentively in John's direction. "Are your parents still abroad?"

"Father is dead and Mother is in Florida, remarried."

"When did your father pass away?" Martin asks.

"Five years ago yesterday. That's life."

"Sameer," Vera says. "Meriam told us your dad passed away recently."

"Yes." Make as short an answer as possible.

"Well, I feel lucky," Richard quips, and looks at his father. "May you live 'til a hundred and twenty."

"Thank you." Martin says, unmoved. "I find childhood memories a constant source of happiness. I still retreat to them when life gets cruel. I bet you're starting to feel that way, John." Martin is pressing him to open up.

"Well, I'm so busy, I haven't yet had the leisure to reminisce."

"That sounds almost sacrilegious," Martin replies.

"I heard a sacrilegious joke," Richard interjects.

"Only if it's clean," Martin says.

"That wouldn't be a joke."

Martin won't take silence for an answer. I am glad I am not one of his students. He looks at John and continues, "Not to belabor the point, but don't you think childhood memories are beautiful?"

"The father who should have given me precious memories never even hugged me with affection, not once." John drops his fork loudly on his plate. "And mind you, I was the one who cared for him every day in the hospital, because Mother had already told him to go to hell."

I have a strange feeling that Richard is nudging John's foot under the table to restrain him.

"Just think of all the freedom from guilt you have because of that," Richard says. "Now you can hate your father and not feel guilty about it. Have some asparagus."

John refuses.

"I may have cooked the asparagus a minute too long," Vera jumps into the middle.

"Everything is extremely delicious, Mother," Meriam says reassuringly.

The conversations now roll into inconsequential dead ends. Academic questions follow. "What do you write? Have published?" "What do you think of…?" Martin keeps the party masked.

I am thinking academics don't know how to enjoy themselves or have fun. I refuse to be part of the game and keep silent. When dinner is over, Martin excuses himself "to take a walk and work in my office." This is what he has been doing ever since Meriam remembers. I welcome the suggestion to go out bar hopping with Meriam, Richard and John.

"Café-hopping to keep it dry," Richard corrects.

Richard packs us into his renovated Cougar. "Wow! It's over. How did it go, sister?"

Outside the house, Richard has a transformed face—more serious and relaxed, his voice quieter. I am struck by the change. Obviously, he puts on a special performance for his parents.

"It went okay." Meriam touches her brother affectionately.

"John, I'm sorry," Richard says.

"They were very polite," John sneers. "Don't ever subject me to this again. Next time I'm coming disguised as a Viking with two horns."

"Your friend is a strong guy," Richard says, ignoring me.

"Just appearance." I always try to dilute compliments.

"My friend is a great guy," Meriam says, and in open defiance snugs by me in the backseat, holds my hand and presses it to her body.

Meriam is forcing us into the open, at least in front of Richard. I hope she knows him well. Do we know our brothers? I am not ready to come out in the open, but the act has a sweet sensation of decadence. I surprise myself, kissing her on the cheek and feeling the thrill of an illicit act.

Illicit acts trail back to my creation. The first one was a small watermelon the size of a grapefruit. I treaded to a meadow full of watermelons in daylight with two other nine year olds. We had hardly picked one before the owner followed us with a barrage of stones and lexicon of curses I'd never heard before. The red melon was still partially white when we opened it, but there was a sweetness to it. I never stole after that. But there is no fretful owner around.

"We should get together more often," Meriam tells Richard and John.

"I'd love that," Richard sounds warm, relaxed and sincere.

"You two should come down to visit us." John looks back at us. "We can go places together—or sit and talk normal.

"Well, why not set a date right away? No misunderstandings, Sameer, this invitation is for you, too. The only thing I share with my father is his allergy to Sam." Richard laughs deeply. At last he sounds himself.

"Oh, stop it, Richard," Meriam says halfheartedly.

"Where shall we go?" he asks me.

"Somewhere real," John answers instead. "Real people, real talk, real dirt and normal conversation. Sorry Meriam, I don't mean to be offensive."

"It's okay. Father isn't like that all the time. He just wants a grandchild. I don't want any." Meriam stops abruptly.

"We would like to adopt a child," Richard glances at John. "If they let us."

"That's not the kind of grandson your father has in mind, dear," John stretches his arm and massages Richard's back.

"Let's show Sameer rural America, outside the tourist line, Martin's line, and the urban line!"

"Great," I say feeling relieved.

Richard drives out of Westport. We stop in front of the Black and White Diner, a large sign announces, "Specializing in steamers, fried clams, and all the fish you can eat."

"Rural America is more than sleazy joints," John tells me. "Once I was interested in Maxim Gorky. I used to go see real people in rural areas. Wrinkled, sloppy, fat and real."

"Why should 'real' be associated with the ugly or poor? Can't real people be rich and drink fine wine?" Meriam tries to jolt us back.

"Maybe because the rich camouflage feelings," I say. "Funny, I used to love Gorky too. I used to go to a certain café in Jaffa. I taught Arabic in a Catholic school there. Couldn't last more than one year. Like Gorky, I thought I'd find real people in simple side-walk cafés. The summer was hot and damp. All I remember is sweaty summers and waiters sprinkling water over the dusty pavements to cool the air, and total numbness from the heat. I thought I was in the midst of real world, simple people until later I discovered my café was a den for hash addicts."

John laughs at my comments. The group has adjusted to each other, the pendulum is balanced.

We enter the diner like two couples that have known each other for a long time.

People make places memorable. A waitress constantly laughing and joking. Just like a farm, the diner has everything it needs - - a make-do bar to the side, a jukebox shaped like a mailbox, a cross with the suffering Christ in one corner.

"That hasn't been dusted since it was mounted," John quips. Meriam is quiet. She sits close to me on a bench and her body clings warmly to mine. Richard and John plan their next day together. John says that Richard shouldn't go to bed too late so he can prepare a brief. John has a meeting, but they will have dinner at 7:00. Richard will fix the salad—John promises a surprise Albanian dish. It's all so quiet.

"We insist you visit us."

"Yes," Meriam reassures her brother.

The morning after the dinner, Vera and Martin are subdued. The experience with John is hashed over at breakfast.

Meriam assures her parents, "Richard is happy."

"How could anybody be happy under those conditions?" With the resignation of a martyr, Martin adds, "I'm confident. No, I suspect my son is intelligent enough to know."

A sense of fate, of kismet, has fallen over the household. My vision is blurred. I do not distinguish lines of destiny. I feel I have been in an emotional whirlpool and I'm anxious to talk to Meriam in private.

The family cordially forces an amiable departure. "We want you to feel at home and come back soon," Martin says. "We didn't have time to discuss the politics of Israel and Palestine," as he waves us out of the driveway.

Meriam's love is a floodlight, pouring straight on my eyes. Her closeness numbs my doubts, and my guilt. Slowly a sweet corruption seeps into me. I am shocked, more by myself than by her. Shocked that I do not ask myself what my mother would say, or my father, or my friends. Her chestnut hair, and olive skin, and green eyes wrap me in clouds of ecstasy.

"How glorious it is to be in love" is our main topic. We repeat it in variations of words, hugs and kisses. I feel as though my chest broadens for the autumn air. After the desolation of my marriage to Christine, Meriam is the real Oasis. Why do I think of the Oasis? The restaurant is only around the next sunset, and so is life with Sam. I press these thoughts down firmly in my mind like the inner shroud of a mummy.

What am I going to do next? The question steals into an anxious corner of my mind. "I should move again, this time both home and employer." I turn to Meriam. "Being away from you will be hell."

"No, please don't. Please don't move out." Meriam touches my face and looks me straight in the eyes.

"But, Sam," at last his name forces itself on us.

"We will manage, like we did so far," Meriam says assuringly.

"I don't know how to face him tomorrow," I say.

"For years Sam has had no problems facing me after his affairs. Please don't reach any decision, we'll manage, you'll see. Try to be fair-minded," she pleads.

Fair mindedness? That was before I was adulterous - - before I betrayed Sam's trust.

As we approach the Massachusetts Turnpike, we see clouds surface. Meriam is entertaining a group of women for lunch. I'll be back to my customers. A strange silence takes over, like the one following ritual bells.

Meriam says, "Let's take the back way home."

"I feel like a drive south instead of north," I say. "All the way to Mexico." An outlaw in a Western movie.

We stretch the day, but cannot stop it. Signs to Newton start appearing as frequently as cooling autumn showers. We enter the driveway, my hands on my side of the car, restrained.

I am ready to go to my room, but Sam wants to debrief us, "I think you deserve a medal for replacing me at the dinner with Richard and

John."

"John is well traveled in the Middle East," I say.

"So are all the retired, wealthy widows of Texas," Sam adds.

"Bigotry, Sam, bigotry." Meriam, coy, finds her way back to her nest.

When I ask Sam about his house guests, "Politics, food and drink—a Zionist orgy," is all I get out of him.

Staying upstairs alone while Meriam is downstairs with Sam strikes me as obscene. I avoid looking at my Hippie Christ in the eyes. I'm not ready for a sermon.

CHAPTER 15

The weekend whirled me far away from grills, waitresses, and stuffed grape leaves. Going back to the Oasis forces a different reality on me.

It's nice to be missed, even for a weekend. Tuesday morning after the Westport weekend, waitresses are attentive. Maybe people in love are likable, for suddenly I feel women are more forward.

At lunch break I sit with Judy, the headwaitress. She has a bumper sticker "Jesus Saves" and now she's wearing a "Jesus Saves" ring. Sam does have an ecumenical staff.

"It's time Jesus saves some Nazarenes," I kid Judy. I'm fascinated by people who go through spiritual rebellions. I sit with Judy to find out about her conversion. I feel like a pagan detective.

We're joined by Jim, a retired businessman who has his lunch daily at the Oasis, and smokes a Havana cigar afterwards. "I can't complain, 83 going on 84." He hums Gershwin tunes on the way in and out of the restaurant. He's my local sage, I barrage him with questions.

"If you were to go through life again, would you change a lot?"

"Not very much, I would have stayed outdoors more. Smelled more flowers, watched more birds. I can't complain," he says with an unusual sense of contentment. Waitresses love him in spite of his cigars.

"It would be easier to convert me than make me give up my cigars," Jim jokes. He seems to live in peace with his 83 years of experience.

Unlike Jim, I'm afraid I'll sleep on spikes until the time I reach 83, spikes rooted in last weekend.

Sam joins us to kibitz with Jim. "What shall I do? My head chef is an Arab, and three of my waitresses are born-again Christians."

"Being reborn is easier than converting to Judaism and the Mikve." Jim is Jewish. "In the Billy Graham Stadium, you convert to the sound of music and a choir of thousands." He chuckles.

"I don't understand people who change their religious light bulbs, do you, Sameer? Why do they do it? I pay them enough," Sam says laughing.

I turn to Judy. "What does it mean to you, to be re-born?"

"It's a long story. We need a whole evening."

I wish I could comprehend the light that led her to another baptism. Is it the same light I am after? The light that sparked me with love?

Nazareth bubbles with Christian missionaries. A Southern Baptist once invited my grandmother to his service. She asked him with sincerity, "But why? I have my church." She has a church. It runs back to Jesus, confined within the city limits. Why should she go to a service of a Baptist from Missouri? The idea puzzled her. A natural spring flows inside her church, our church—legend has it flowing since the time of the Holy Family.

In the following days, I feel the mugginess of deception on my chest. But all mugginess disappears whenever I'm close to Meriam. We rake leaves together. She closes her eyes, draws me to her. The usually serene Meriam is out of control. But who wants control? I enjoy seeing this side of her.

Like swimmers, every time we are together we dare each other to dive deeper. The desire that erupted on the weekend drives us into each other's arms in the corners of the house. And the house is very large - - even by Newton standards.

CHAPTER 16

Events accelerate like non sequiturs. "Non sequitur" is a word I picked up from Martin, and it appeals to my sense of absurdity. I have the whole Sunday off, except for the evening shift at five.

First, I get a telephone call from Richard while I'm lounging on the living room couch reading The Sunday Globe. "Is Meriam there?"

"No, both of them are out."

"She arrived!" Richard says excitedly.

"What?" I ask him.

"Nicole arrived," he shouts.

"Who's Nicole?"

"Our new baby," he says. Silence.

"Baby?" I ask politely.

"My baby," he repeats. "We kept it as a surprise. A friend with an unwanted pregnancy named me as the father! She knew we wanted a baby. She almost delivered the baby to my arms. I was even at the hospital. It's only a case of custody, not adoption. You've got to come with Meriam to see her. She's beautiful. Our neighbors with a one-year-old son are talking marriage! We already have to protect her. John wants me to get some sleep, but I'm sitting here wide awake. I've never been so wide awake in my life. I thought it was about time you got up."

I congratulate him and encourage him to rest, then hang up. It's noon. Will Nicole be happy? I am still lying on the couch when, suddenly, all I see is a huge bosom and a defiant face standing over me with a suitcase still in her hand.

"Who the hell are you?"

"Who are you?" I answer back.

"Esther," she says.

I look around to see if she brought the husband Sam hopes for. No one is around but me. "I don't believe they know you're coming," I say.

"U.C.L.A. has a short vacation. I didn't think I need clearance to come to my own home," Esther snaps.

Before I can blink, the doorbell rings and Riyad is at the door, a surprise visit from Brown University. "If Mohammed doesn't come to the mountain, the mountain comes to Mohammed! Sameer, where the hell were you all this time? I counted six kosher delicatessens on the way here. You might as well be living in Tel-Aviv."

Riyad towers over Esther. His black eyes scan her breasts, bringing red embarrassment to my face. Riyad, my childhood friend, hasn't changed since we used to chase girls together in adolescence. His sensuality still marches ahead of him.

"This is Riyad," I say to Esther.

"This is who?" Esther asks.

The rudeness of Esther's question only inflames Riyad. "I don't read this as a cordial greeting."

"Riyad, this is Esther," I introduce them. The fact that Esther is a Jewish name adds mischief to Riyad's cynicism, and suddenly I think of the Encyclopedia Judaica on the bookshelves.

"What is Sam doing, turning this house into a P.L.O. branch?" Esther asks.

"I consider that a compliment, madam." Riyad's eyes widen.

"It depends," Esther answers back.

I start explaining to Esther. "As a matter of fact, I live in your room." I turn to Riyad. "I apologize for not contacting you after I left Christine."

Both of them now have the same question unanswered. I can read it in their eyes. "Why on earth did you move in here?" they ask, almost in unison.

I don't have a guardian angel. I lost her along the way, but the arrival of Sam and Meriam amounts to one.

Sam kisses Esther, "Did you flunk out of school?" As soon as Sam hears the news about Nicole, he starts laughing. Nobody can keep a serious face around his laughter. Meriam calls Richard immediately.

"You must have a drink, Riyad," Sam insists. "We must celebrate the birth of my niece."

"No, let's have lunch together. You will have lunch with us, Riyad. Please do." Meriam is ignoring Esther. "Why don't you and Sameer catch up on news, and we'll call you when it's ready."

Upstairs, Riyad is unimpressed. "You seem to be cushioned in comfort. Have you forgotten?" His notorious temperament is showing.

"Forgotten what?"

"What they have done to us."

"Of course not," I say. Anthony caught in the act of treason in Cleopatra's powder room. Betrayal is soaked with delusions. Have I stopped seeing?

"Do they know about the prisons in Israel?" Riyad looks at me and I glance outside. Manicured backyards, maple trees and lawns stretch undisturbed by war. Newton, Massachusetts.

Of course, I remember. The soldiers lined us up under the blazing sun in the jail yard until we saw hazy circles, then we didn't see at all. We were thrown into a cell fuming with the smell of crushed bugs. Riyad, nine other teachers and I were arrested for nothing, except asking for equal pay.

"I don't see the connection," I say.

"For us, everything is connected."

"That's paranoia."

"God damn it, Sameer," Riyad starts in.

"You lose your logic when you get this hot-headed. You have to show both sides - - be objective." I try to calm him.

"With your kind of reason we lose. We need money and patriotism. Israel took the Golan Heights and kept it. The West Bank and kept it. Jerusalem and kept it. Do you think Jordan and Syria need to be more objective? Damn it, Sameer, this won't be solved in middle-class suburbs.

"Are you questioning my loyalty?"

Riyad looks at me, eyebrows still knotted from his vehement speech. "No."

I sigh. "Okay, what's going on?"

Riyad notices the enlargement of my father's picture. "Sameer, your father is the reason I came. Your father lived a good life." He hugs me consoling. We both sit looking in opposite directions, our vision misty. I remember Father telling us, "Take good care of each other, you are like brothers." Suddenly, it's a reunion. I'm a Christian. Riyad is a Muslim. Just like brothers.

"Ya…Zaim," Riyad says, calling me by my childhood nickname, Leader. "Tell me all about it, who are these people? Sam has it up here," Riyad points to his nose. "And Esther all up here," pointing to his chest. "And Meriam here," pointing to his butt - - a cute, attractive detail I'd have to admit.

"Jesus, is that all you see in people?" I ask him.

"That should tell you something about my current state of mind." Then abruptly he asks, "How's Christine?"

"Christine?" I'm embarrassed. "What is there to know? We're divorced."

"She is educated, she loves you, and she's pretty. What more do you want?"

"You haven't been married."

"I haven't been in a cloister either."

"You're right about Christine."

"Then why?"

"It's the small fly that destroys the flavor of a dish."

"Is that all that you can see in a wife?" Riyad throws a boomerang.

"It's the mosquito that disturbs your sleep."

"You mean to tell me you divorced for trivial reasons?"

"I mean to tell you that trivial things are part of life. It's like a junk sale, everything is there and gets jumbled together."

"You're still a lousy philosopher." Riyad is upset but eager to talk. "You haven't told me anything about these people."

"Sam is my boss at the restaurant. Meriam is his wife. Esther is his daughter from a previous marriage."

"That's all?"

"That's all."

"Do you really want to eat kosher food downstairs?"

"I cook in his restaurant. Do you think they eat kosher food?"

"What's this cooking all about? Aren't you going back to teaching?"

"No, and they were nice to me. First, I thought he wouldn't hire somebody as a cook who's a teacher and a Palestinian. Then, later, it never came up. How are your studies going?"

"Great, except that one of my profs is a Zionist, and in poli sci, he can't hide his real opinions."

"Can you hide yours?"

"No, and I don't want to. I'm proud of who I am. Proud of my culture - - food, music, poetry, values, family, proud of it all."

So am I. Suddenly, Riyad sounds more convincing.

I put on an album of Feiruz. Music binds us with threads of nostalgia, songs about girls gathering around the village fountain, and boys in love.

We go down to lunch, but I'm not totally comfortable. Riyad is wearing a T-shirt with a map of Palestine on it, and I sense Esther has decided to assert her Jewishness. We sit down in the living room. Esther has changed clothes, and also put on a pout the size of a thunderstorm.

"Dad works too hard, Sameer," Esther says as she massages Sam's shoulders.

Her tone sounds more like, "Dad works too hard - - and Meriam works too little." Somehow I feel on guard.

"Sam doesn't believe that the Lord rested on the seventh day," I say.

"It's good the Lord wasn't subject to collective bargaining. He would have rested the whole week if it was up to the unions," Sam quips.

"Dad, you're still a bigot."

"My Lord works at night on term papers," Riyad says and moves over by Esther on the couch. Meriam's still out in the kitchen.

"Let me guess," Esther turns toward Riyad, tucking her legs under her. "You must be writing on an Arabic topic." She's obviously Sam's daughter.

"I better see if I can help Meriam," preferring not to be around when they clash. Meriam often asks me to put the final touches on her dishes. I usually use the colorful fruits and vegetables - - radishes, grapes, green peppers for decoration. Visual seduction.

"Esther is staying in the guest room downstairs," Meriam whispers to me. "Sam's littler daughter, they have a special relationship, basically one of daughter manipulating father. She's a Jewish American Princess, down to the bottom or her cleavage. Did you see how she dresses? I think she finds Riyad attractive." Meriam shakes her head with a suspended smile. "She's going out with Sam later." Her arm brushes softly on mine.

I move a bit backwards, and go to join the others. Sam is busy at the bar pouring a glass of Arak for Riyad.

"This guy could pass for an Arab. He has the real stuff in his bar," Riyad says.

"I suppose that's meant to be a compliment." Esther doesn't believe in closing her eyes, ears, or mouth. The pout has disappeared from her face. The three of them are drinking Arak. Nobody pouts while downing Arak.

The dish Meriam serves is a favorite - - ground lamb spread over sautéed eggplant and pine nuts with saffron rice to the side. For the salad, she made tabouli, an extravaganza of colorful vegetables in red and green, mixed with bulgar and served on romaine lettuce leaves.

"You expected gefilte fish, I suppose," Sam says passing the eggplant to an obviously surprised Riyad.

"Sameer's influence," Meriam looks at me smiling.

"The best conversion takes place around food, but don't worry, Zionists are too racist to be missionaries." Sam's eyes are twinkling.

"You're right. The Sermon on the Mount happened after a huge fish dinner," Riyad says.

I'm amused he remembers anything from the New Testament.

"In the U.S. we have Christian soup kitchens." Esther doesn't miss a dig.

"If you mean the Salvation Army, they really do a good job," Riyad says seriously.

"That's a point of view." Esther shakes her head.

"That's a point of hunger." Riyad pours himself more Arak, adds water, turning it milk-white.

"It's a disgrace that we still have poor people who need Salvation Army soup kitchens. The government should help the poor," Esther says.

"These are not my ideas," Sam says to Riyad. "They're her mother's, I'm sure. My ex is the size of a woodpecker and creates the same amount of noise." Sam gives Esther a patronizing pat.

"Watch out, Dad."

I can see Sam is becoming sentimental. I wondered what two strong Araks would do to him.

"You're okay, hon." Turning to us, he continues, "She used to be the sweetest kid."

"Sweet," Esther sneers, "Yuk."

"She still is," Riyad's overt move almost makes me choke. Where sex and politics conflict, Riyad makes an exception for himself.

"Well, so are you," Esther rises to the challenge. Meriam's face flashes a knowing smile.

"When she was nine, she wrote me a letter asking me to come back. I'll never forget it. That's the only time I had tears over divorcing the woodpecker." Sam is definitely getting sentimental.

"I don't remember anything," Esther says.

"I still keep it, I'll show you." Sam goes off to fetch the letter. Meriam follows him.

Riyad looks at me and says in Arabic, "She sure has a body."

When he returns, Sam flashes the letter in Riyad's face. The letter written on a sheet of lined paper, crammed together in child-like order.

Dear Sam Weinstein,
If you come back and live with us, I will,

STOP SPITTING,
I WILL NOT COME IN WHEN YOU ARE SLEEPING,
I WON'T FIGHT WITH MATTY WHEN YOU ARE SLEEPING,
I WON'T FIGHT WITH YOU
I WILL DO WHAT YOU SAY,
I WILL DO WHAT I AM TOLD.

And if I have done anything else wrong I will do it if you tell me to. And I will not mistreat you.

PLEASE COME BACK AND LIVE WITH US.
BY ESTHER WEINSTEIN

"My God," Esther covers her face. "You're embarrassing me."

"It's touching." Riyad looks at Esther.

"That's my Esther." Sam stands tall and proud like a decorated

Christmas tree. He hugs her and plants a resounding kiss on her cheek.

"We're a hugging family," Esther tells Riyad.

"Arabs love to hug too, don't we, Sameer? Your letter to Sam is heartbreaking." Riyad looks straight at Esther.

"So, you have a sentimental side?"

"I spent years trying to forget about that letter," Esther says.

Esther has an animal charm. She sits in complete comfort, legs attractively tanned, her breasts in the way of her sentences. Riyad is finding it difficult to control his eyes. When the mind is used to undressing the opposite sex, it is difficult to stop. I am glad I'm sitting next to Riyad, where I don't have to look directly at Esther.

"You said you forgot your letter?" Sam's face clouds.

"I wanted to forget the letter, because I remember your refusal," Esther says. "A young woman comes and steals your father, try to respect men after that. Men. Their hard-ons have no conscience. She swept him off his feet."

I'm sure Riyad is not used to hearing a woman talk like this. He laughs nervously.

"You see, Sameer," Sam says. "Give women free expression and they abuse it."

"She swept you away, admit it."

"<u>She</u> has a name," Sam says. Meriam is in the kitchen getting dessert.

"Men need to be at least seven years older in order to control a woman," Riyad declares.

"Dad, you have fifteen years and I'm not sure you succeeded."

"Esther, damn it." Sam tries to stop her.

"Now I come home and find my room occupied."

"Time to find a husband." Sam tries to detonate an explosive.

"I'm sorry about the room," I rush to say.

"Don't take it personally, Sameer, it's just the principle of it. Men

92

have children and dump them in women's laps."

"This is changing," I say. "Men are sharing custody."

"A token. It will never be 50/50."

"Would you rather have stayed with me?" Sam says.

"And lived with her?"

Thank God Meriam is not at the table.

"Her name is Meriam." Sam turns to Riyad. "Esther is presenting you with the saga of Sam Weinstein. We always go through this family drama on her first day home. Well, Esther," Sam continues, "There's the challenge. You can be a better parent someday."

Meriam comes in with a fruit dessert, a "papaya special." I am anticipating the worst.

"You screw up the world and then expect the kids to fix it," Esther snaps back.

"You're getting a baptism in Jewish, free-style, father-daughter haggling," Meriam tells me. "I'll bet Arab daughters act differently with their fathers."

"It's more an attitude of respect and support," Riyad says.

"Subjugation and slavery," Esther corrects him.

"Esther, I think you're drinking too much." Meriam sounds firm.

"Now wait a minute," Riyad stands up. "If my sister talked like this to my father, I'd be the one who'd slap her face."

"So, you also beat your women?" Esther says to Riyad, ignoring Meriam's comment.

"That's where you're wrong. We beat the man who beats his wife." Riyad is indignant. "Honor is important. Nobility of character," he says standing up, getting more intense.

"Weren't those values found in Europe in the dark Ages?" Esther asks calmly.

"You'd make a wonderful couple," Sam kids Riyad. "A typical lovers' quarrel."

"I don't buy your style of equality!" Riyad sits down, glaring at Esther. "Women in your 'liberated' system are losing out. I want progress and technology, but I want it to fit my culture, my traditions. American culture brought rape, crime, incest and drugs." Turning to Meriam, Riyad continues, "Do you know how I felt when I first came to the U.S.? That the whole country was a patch of mushrooms—on the surface and without roots, the newer the better."

"I'm for liberation, not abuse," Meriam says.

"Do you know what liberation is doing for men?" Sam asks. "Impotence. Men need porno magazines to live with liberated women."

"And do you know what liberation is bringing women?" Esther raises her voice. "Equal salaries. Legal rights. The men you're talking about can get lost as far as I'm concerned. I believe in good jobs and equality before nobility of character."

"What's wrong with stressing character instead of greed? Your tenant and I were discussing this topic when we were only fourteen," Riyad points in my direction.

"And what did Sameer think then?" Meriam cuts in.

"He was just as bad then as he is today, a mixture of sentimentalism and logic."

"Sam's been a good father." Meriam reaches for Sam's hand affectionately. "That's exactly why I don't want children. The returns are not always satisfying," she says with a twinkle.

"If I expect a Father's Day card, I'm being possessive," Sam says.

"I'm sorry, Dad. Actually I'm happy, and you're the greatest."

"I think I'd better be leaving," Riyad says. "There's an Arabic saying: Don't intrude between the onion and its skin."

"Do we smell that bad?" Sam stands to refill Riyad's drink. "Stay, please do." Sam likes Riyad. After lunch Sam asks me if I can come to the Oasis early, he's short-handed.

In a way, I'm glad I have to go to work. I tell Riyad he can rest in my room.

Esther looks at Riyad and Sam. "Let's talk about something more exciting."

"Yes," Sam agrees.

"I'm thinking of transferring from U.C.L.A. to the Boston area. What do you know about the schools? I'm debating between B.U. and Brandeis." Esther looks at Riyad, with unmistaken sincerity.

"Holy Moses," Sam says. "Let's go to work and get some money for the Brandeis tuition."

The Oasis is full of customers; our banquet room is set up for a wedding. My kitchen area is open, so I can see that the circular booths in the main dining room and the bar section are all crowded.

I like my work - - the fresh feel of lettuce leaves, the promising look of a steaming dish, the tart taste of a properly groomed radish. The spices in the Palestinian kitchen mix and blend like moods of people. The aroma of a dessert carries a different promise than steaming stuffed lamb. Customers who don't see or smell should gulp diet food from cans. There's a counter adjacent to my kitchen area where our regulars usually sit and talk to me.

I favor customers who are cheerful, who savor food and conversation. I'm impatient with glum ones. Is it because I am in love? Meriam has washed my eyes with expectations. Christine's love was different, reliable and comprehensive, but never cheerful. Somehow Christine has slowly been obscured in the quicksand of memory.

I call Riyad several times, curious about the scene I left at home, but no one answers. After a busy evening, I return home to find his car gone, the place dark and quiet except for the rustle of autumn leaves.

At 2:00 a.m. my phone rings. Riyad screams, "I tell you, Sameer, Esther is a female macho."

I struggle to awaken. "Tell me more, what happened?"

"You missed the best part."

"Sam?"

"The Arak took care of Sam. He's wild. He wants me to tell him more about our problems."

"Why doesn't Sam ask me?" Aren't I an Arab in Sam's eyes?

Riyad continues, "His wife is very nice."

"Yes," I say in a neutral voice. I'm not ready to discuss Meriam with Riyad.

"Did you see the way Esther was eyeing me?"

I'm relieved Riyad drops the topic of Meriam. "How far did it go?"

"Far enough to meet again. We fought and made up all night long."

I glance at the clock. "So, I'll be seeing more of you."

Lowering his voice, Riyad says, "If you can't beat them in the battle, you beat them in bed. We'll beat them in battle too. I'm sure about that."

"In bed, Riyad? But don't you surrender at the end?"

"Battles should be won," he declares, obviously exalted by the results of his first engagement.

"Where is Esther now?"

"In your house somewhere, I suppose."

"Am I going to see you soon?"

"Sure," Riyad says.

"You should have stayed here overnight. It must have been a long drive back to Providence."

"Never felt more awake; she's staying for a week," Riyad says, and hangs up.

I fall asleep immediately.

CHAPTER 17

Meriam has her own agenda, an agenda dictated by love. She awakens me at midnight, or in the early morning with a touch of a bare arm or gentle pressure of her body, with whispers of "Sam just left, you're so warm." Today, totally unexpected she whispers, "Today we're going to see Nicole."

I'm being carried like a passive sailboat, and I am enjoying the drift. Nicole becomes the target of our new adventure. Sam is relieved he doesn't need to see Richard—or John.

"You'll have to adjust to your new position of relative in residence," Sam tells me.

It's a relief to be outside without Esther or Sam breathing down our necks. We stop at the first motel in Connecticut after the border on Highway 89. Meriam starts taking off her nylons in the car. The room is sterile, with pictures of a farm and a sunset. Meriam brings a picnic basket of fruit and wine with crystal glasses, a candle, and she slips into nothing. The candle glow fills the room - - conversations are delayed.

Our intimacy has acquired its own simplicity, carrying Miri to bed, taking time for conversation later. Her cheeks become more velvety, her eyes more fixed, her mouth even softer. She starts talking to me, the love talk that cannot be transferred, words that have magic only to my ears. Before, we used to discuss ideas. Now, we focus more on our intimacy. She leads me gently into pleasing her. Steaming with passion, we are excited by the aroma of our love. Our feelings become phrases of exaltation. Language and life - - they share the same root.

Reluctantly, we blow out the candle, dress, then quickly undress again, get dressed and then slip back to the car.

Richard and John live in a small country town, just inland of Westport, on the other side from Martin and Vera. After a telephone call along the way we finally manage to locate them. It is a small farmhouse with a barn and a breathtaking garden of zinnias, asters and hollyhocks.

We find Richard and John listening to harpsichord music. An Italian looking woman tiptoes around them. Josie is Nicole's babysitter. The living room is furnished in Middle-Eastern style, cushions and throw pillows. Meriam wants to see Nicole. We walk through the kitchen, where frying pans hang on the wall above an old-fashioned iron stove. Upstairs on Nicole's door there's a handwritten poster, "Nicole's Power Starts Here!" We step into a child's world of "creative" wooden toys and nonhazardous stuffed animals. I find myself checking to see if there is anything out of the ordinary, but it's like a nursery in any home. The color of the room is the only defiance - - it's blue.

I don't know what to say when faced with babies. In Nazareth there are several things I should say if it were a boy. If it's a girl, you wish the parents "A bridegroom next time." If a girl follows the birth of several boys, you tell the parents, "She is the final crown for her brothers." After that, you don't press you luck.

But Nicole looks sweet, her eyes alert over a pudgy nose and chin.

"She already looks like me, doesn't she?" John asks Meriam.

The babysitter, standing proudly to the side with her hands in her apron, protests, "No, Johnny, she's much prettier."

"Yesterday Josie wrapped Nicole up like an Egyptian mummy. Josie told us it was to keep her bones straight," Richard says.

Josie takes her heavy hands out of her apron and swirls around. "You can see that custom didn't hurt me."

"You should've seen the puzzled look on Nicole's face when we unwrapped her." John puts Nicole in Meriam's arms.

Meriam rests Nicole's head gently on her bosom, her face lights up. Women's faces light up for babies like no man's face can. On the other hand, John and Richard's faces are beaming. I wonder to myself if Martin and Vera had this delight when Richard was born.

Later, downstairs, John tells us all about Nicole's sleeping and eating habits. Like all babies, Nicole edges herself into the conversations, becoming the focus of existence in the living room.

"She is a great baby. Even her burping at the end of a meal is delightful." John looks at Richard for agreement and adds, "We're lucky to have Josie."

"You embarrass me," Josie says and leaves to fix dinner.

"She's a fantastic babysitter. She lives with her brother on a nearby farm. She believes that if you kill a spider in the morning, it's bad luck," Richard says laughing.

Josie, a single woman in her late forties who carries the affection of a thousand generations of Italian mothers, serves us dinner in the living room on large trays. Baked cod marinated in vermouth with tomato slices and big chunks of Italian bread.

"So how's having a baby?" Miri asks her brother.

"Ask Josie," Richard says.

"It's not lonely anymore," Josie says. "Nicole's a happy baby. She makes me wish I'd gone through it myself." An uncontrolled smile and virginal blush flood her open face.

When she leaves the room, Richard whispers, "We wanted a woman who would love Nicole, not psychoanalyze her."

"Or psychoanalyze us," John adds.

John turns on a tape of Arabic music, then stands, flicks his fingers—long, thin, powerful - - and stomps the floor like a Spanish dancer to the Arabic music. Rather than approach Miri, he looks at Richard. "Richardo," he calls with affection, "I'll teach you to belly dance. Sameer, you teach Meriam."

"Oh, no," Meriam says, "I'm too self-conscious to dance."

I take her hand and gently pull her up.

"It's simple, Meriam," Richard says. "Try to seduce Sameer, while dancing."

"That part I like." Meriam presses her lips together in sweet determination. "How are Arabs seduced?"

"Easily," I whisper. I slide my hand gently over her hair. "From here all the way down to the toes, your eyes, your neck, your waist, everything in you seduces me." I dance in front of her. "You move towards me as I come towards you," a hundred memories of weddings in my mind. Father dancing gracefully with Mother, the boys dancing with temptation, our minds fixed on a girl in the crowd. Belly dancing frees repressed desires. Desires become transparent in a curve of a mouth, or shake of the breasts.

Miri shakes her body - - a bit more than an Arab woman would - - while John and Richard dance in circles. John mesmerizes Richard and dances around him; he bends back—all the way to the floor. They must have danced before.

In Nazareth, men dance together. They hold hands and move together in a string of half circles, a union tied like rosary beads. They stomp their feet and jump high. They dance and swirl scarves, with the others circling around them. And they call on each other to "warm it up," creating a trail of masculine heat. It is a dancing ode, the body's ode to the soul.

We settle down, reclining on cushions, two intimate couples. John nestles by Richard and Miri by me. I wonder if two married couples could be this happy. Do I see right from wrong?

"We have to introduce you to our ducks," Richard announces.

"Don't tell me my brother raises ducks in his free time."

"No, not those kind of ducks," Richard sounds happy. He goes to the other room and brings back an armful of duck hunting decoys. He holds up one and says, "Please meet Dracula Duck." It's black and a chain hangs from its side. He holds up another. "This is Sir Francis Drake Duck. And this is Titanic Duck, he sinks. Here is Cork Duck, he's made of cork. And here's Very Late Night Duck. And, last, this is Happy New Year Drink Duck, he can't sit up straight. We collected them from yard sales."

The ducks cheer us and Meriam is amused. John and Richard have created their own dream world - - as Meriam and I have. We are both hiding in a dream, and I pray that it will last through the brightness of sunlight.

"Have you talked with Dad about Nicole?" Miri asks.

"Dad muttered and stuttered." Richard peels a red delicious apple. "Dad needs to research the question before he takes a stand on it." A chilled smile of hurt freezes on his face.

"And Mom?"

"Well," Richard's face relaxes, "you know Mom, she usually has two stands - - one for Dad and one for us."

"I talked to Vera," John interrupts Richard. "We had a prim and proper conversation. 'A parcel is in the mail' she told me."

Although Martin and Vera live on the other side of town, the distance hangs between them like a broken bridge.

"So many family complications," Miri sighs.

I'm wondering if she includes us in that statement.

"There's a lot you don't know," John says. "Martin's anger at dinner really hit me. That's why I decided to make up the stereotypes he wanted. So I invented them, my cold father, my domineering mother."

"Oh, John, you shouldn't have," Miri says.

"John's father is gentle and kind and so is his mother," Richard explains anxiously.

"You mean that was all a lie?" Miri is smiling now.

"That was an act," Richard corrects her. "John will spend the coming years trying to correct it." He sounds more amused than upset.

Meriam suddenly looks to the side and dries a tear.

"Meriam loves you a lot," Richard turns to me, for the first time confronting me with my relation to his sister.

"When I'm this happy." Miri's eyes smile through her tears. "I want it to last, but guilt creeps in."

"Wow," Richard says. "My dear sister, why push guilt into it?"

"Sometimes I think of morality. I have nagging questions I have to settle with myself." She looks at me, "Sorry, Sameer."

"Public morality stinks," Richard says. "I found that out a long time ago. There are very few standards that are worth living up to. The system is corrupt to the bone."

"If you betray each other's trust, how would you accommodate that morally?" I am thinking of Sam but speak with detachment.

"I'd break his neck - - or mine," Richard bursts out.

"There are many products in the morality store," John says. "Just don't pick Sam's or Martin's."

Meriam laughs. "Sameer is Sameer and nobody else. That's why I love him. I spend a lot of time pulling out the arrows he's shot at himself."

"Really," John says. "That's really wild imagery."

"But answer Sameer's question about trust," Meriam insists.

"It won't happen to us," Richard answers instead. "We won't stay together if he betrays me. We spend many nights talking. We live outside public morality, but you're in the thick of it with Sam, and our parents. Meriam, people are born needy, and they spend their lives fulfilling their needs or starving. If you try to satisfy those needs according to public morality, you starve. Live up to your personal morals, and you suffer on the public front." He pauses, then adds abruptly, "You've crossed political boundaries, I've crossed moral boundaries. Which is easier?"

"I think I have crossed both," I say. I sound like my Hippie Christ.

Richard continues, "Just the hypocrisy of it. Go to a supermarket and you're barraged by the 'how to' public morality - - and how to keep a marriage, screw a woman, love a cat. The only thing I understand is me. That's where my morality starts and ends."

Nicole's scream puts an end to our conversation. In a way I am relieved. Centering on Nicole's tears and reflexes is simpler, fresher and purer than centering on us. We do not return to the topic of faith and trust.

Only once does Richard ask Meriam, "What does Sam think you're doing today anyhow, picking strawberries?"

"Visiting you," Meriam answers, putting a dull end to his funny line.

When we leave Richard and John, it is dark and cool. The darkness has taken over like obsessive nightmares.

"The issues of trust and honesty are the hardest ones for me," Meriam says as she moves close to me in the spacious seat. I am driving.

"Sameer, help me, say something."

"You're right. It's true, and there are no answers. I guess we have to deal with it as a matter of fact, like the germs we touch every day without knowing."

"If you ever betray me, don't tell me, I'd be shattered," Meriam says. "I must sound crazy."

Meriam seems to forget that at the other end of this drive, she'll end up in the same bed with Sam. I don't. Jealousy frames the mind, and I am terrified of its invasion.

I change the subject. "Esther is at the other end, how are you going to handle her?"

"If she's going to be walking around half naked, I'm going to drape her with a blanket." Meriam gently tidies my hair and adds, "At home, Esther is only interested in her father. I'm simply a threat."

"I'm glad she's returned with so many social causes. She'll see less of us," I try to joke.

"It's only for a week. She always shows up around her birthday. She comes and goes. Sam calls her Hurricane Esther. She'll be bringing her friends to the Oasis and charging it on the tab. Sam calls the table where she sits the non-profit table."

We laugh. Sam is never too far, and his humor is with us.

"I'm morally corrupt, I think. I don't fight it anymore. Maybe I'm getting it in small doses - - like snake poison—just enough to immunize myself. What if I become totally immune and totally corrupt?"

We drive back in silence. I hope I am moral. If I am immoral, I hope the immorality doesn't seep inside my soul and color it, like a drop of black ink.

CHAPTER 18

Like a patient with a rare illness reading medical texts, I start reading books on sex and adultery. The books offer numbers. If I am age thirty, I probably do it a certain number of times per month. I read frequencies of sexual intercourse by age, sex and income. Sociological statistics sound like the inventory of a whorehouse getting ready for accreditation. I'm afraid to look into psychology.

I start watching Sam, trying to guess who his mistresses are. I detect some clues - - a fresh shower not taken at home, an unusual brush of his hair, women who come and sit in special observation posts at the restaurant.

Slowly the question writhes its way from the back of my mind and fills it. Is Sam aware? Does he notice or doesn't he? My curiosity about the other side of Meriam, the one Sam shares, starts eroding our intimacy. Do they make love? Do they talk about me?

Miri says it was difficult for her before and now it's worse. But her friendship and empathy for Sam has not dwindled. I start to acquire the sorting eyes of a critical outsider who's desperately sifting feelings in search of the elusive grain of truth.

But Meriam is in love, and my day is interrupted by love notes everywhere - - under my pillow, between my sheets, on my desk, on the mirror. Meriam finds her way into the hidden corners of my life. She wants to carry me to her universe coated in pink clouds.

Ten days after Esther's arrival, Sam takes me aside. We've got to do something special. It's Esther's birthday. I've invited Riyad."

"You think they can overcome their political conflicts?" I ask.

"They already have. Esther is discovering the Arabic cuisine. She insisted on having the dinner here." He points to a center table with a "reserved" sign. "She went through a Swedish stage two years ago. She got into that one so deeply, I almost had to build a sauna. I feel responsible for her, though maybe guilt is a better word. Meriam's coming too. She didn't want to offend Esther on her birthday."

I feel embarrassed. Neither Riyad nor Meriam has seen me on duty. Arabs don't value cooking as an occupation for men. Riyad and I dreamed of careers as "men of letters."

At age eleven I wanted to escape to dreams. I almost ran away to a dream.

One evening in the midst of summer when there is a big moon over the Galilee, I'm running away to a monastery. I leave home with a note to my family that I love them, and go. I know there is a monastery on Mount Tabor by the Sea of Galilee where I can hide, watch the sun set, dream and write. Dusk comes followed by a big moon. Shepherds are returning to villages and guard dogs surround them. Shepherds' flutes. Screams from a distance asking, "Who are you?" echo across the valleys. Grass is dry, thorns are all that's left. I lose my way, I go back home, hoping they didn't see the note. Mother sees through me, gives me a cup of cocoa and rushes me to a warm bed before Father returns from a futile search. Life goes on next morning.

Every time I run into a dream I bang my head on a wall. At 12, I rush to a Catholic church in Nazareth. I tell the priest, a portly man with big wise eyes and flushed cheeks, that I want to be a monk. I had never entered a Catholic church before. The priest knows my family. There are several thousand of them in the Galilee. We are Greek Orthodox. Our church flows back to early Christianity. Sometimes I forget I'm talking about Nazareth.

"Why do you want to become a Catholic? Why do you want to join a monastery?" I tell him that God is the same for all, that I like to read and write.

He knows things I don't. If he accepts me, my family will storm his church. Nazareth will be rioting. In Nazareth people grow within religions, they don't convert to them. Father Angelo gives me a book of prayers - - black cover with a golden cross. "Read it," he says, "learn it by heart before you come again."

My heart is closed to learning by heart. I am insulted by his cold reception. I see myself as a monk, but not a monk that chants ready-made prayers. I want to write my own. I go home and burn the book and burn the dream with it. Riyad and I continue to grow up and dream, and Israel nudges us off our most precious dream, our homeland.

Sam arrives with Riyad, Esther and Meriam. Judy, the hostess, gives them the royal treatment. I stand by their table to great them, uncomfortable, feeling my inner face is being washed out in the open. The table is set for four and is surrounded by tall plants.

"Sameer, you should join us for a drink." Meriam points to a chair. I pull it to the table.

"Sure, Sameer, relax. Both your helpers are here tonight," Sam moves his chair so that I can sit comfortably between Meriam and him.

The music has started. Sam escorts Esther for the first dance. He looks more in harmony with Esther than I've ever seen him with Meriam. Even in height. He's taller than Esther, but Meriam towers above him.

Riyad aggravates me by saying in Arabic, "Don't worry, our armies will prevail."

Meriam asks for a translation. I have to lie. "It's a nice place," I translate. Why are petty lies more embarrassing than grand ones?

Sam and Esther return laughing from the dance floor. Judy, the hostess, rushes over to tell Sam there is a determined lady claiming to have reserved this very table. I glance toward the door. A woman, hair to her waist, looks in our direction fuming. She's talking to a bald, but heavily bearded man. I've seen her before. She often sits here and Sam always joins her.

"Invite them to the bar," Sam says. "Sameer will take care of them. I'm busy now. Read to her from the Scriptures if you have to."

"Sameer, I forgot to show you where I left tomorrow's menu." I know the menu. Sam showed it to me. I quickly realize that Sam wants to tell me something in private and follow him to the open kitchen.

"Sameer, Janice is her name." Sam talks fast, a look of suspended anticipation around his mouth.

"Who's Janice?"

"Janice is a sexy, possessive, temperamental woman. I'd vote for banning guns just so she would never have access to one. You're lucky she hasn't discovered you yet. Do me a favor, seat her on the other side, a distant table. Stay with her. Discuss politics with her. Chain her to the chair. Please do anything, but keep her away from me while Meriam is here."

"Of course," I say, wondering whether Meriam would really be jealous of this woman.

"And Esther is very protective when it comes to women," Sam adds as we walk back to the table.

Sam takes Meriam to dance. Esther remains with Riyad. I am left alone, another inner face gets scalded in reality. It hurts. I realize I have let myself slide. I can't appear with myself in public.

I walk to the bar to pacify Janice. "We owe you an apology, ma'am, about your reservation. I am Sameer, Mr. Weinstein's assistant."

"I know who you are." Janice opens her wide blue eyes to look at me more closely.

"We'll have the corner by the palm trees ready for you soon," I tell her.

"But that's in the back of the restaurant. I'll stay here and wait until you clean my usual table. Clear those people out." Janice points to Sam's table.

Her cheeks are high, her hair thick, waving around like a fisherman's net. I wonder why she let her hair grow down to the waist. A strong distraction like that is intended to hide something.

"This is Bill," she says pointing to her companion, who is gulping a beer. Bill tries to laugh, then wipes his mouth and his long, thin, pointed nose. His small eyes look watery.

"A drink on the house," I tell Susan, the bartender.

"One alcoholic in the family is enough," Janice says and looks with disgust at Bill, who ignores her comment and continues to wipe his nose. "You can ask me to dance instead of apologizing."

Before I can respond, Janice is leading me to the dance floor where Sam, Meriam, Esther and Riyad are all dancing.

Riyad passes us and asks in Arabic, "Who is this piece?"

"God knows," I answer. I roll my eyes with resignation.

Sam gives me a grin. Esther looks at me, her eyes saying, "That was fast." I avoid Meriam's eyes. Janice has both arms around me.

"We have drinks waiting," I say steering Janice back to the bar.

"The drinks can wait. You're a good dancer. Who's your boss dancing with?"

"His wife."

"His wife," Janice repeats. "That son of a bitch. Isn't he separated? Are you married too?"

"No." I don't want to discuss Sam and Meriam with Janice. I can feel her powerful temperament in her impulsive tight hug, in her eyes and lips.

"What's the matter, are you afraid of women?" she asks me. In a move intended to make Sam jealous, she tightens her grip on my body and kisses my neck.

"Hey, wait a minute," I say. "We barely know each other."

"I know you better than you think."

"Our kitchen is in open view. Customers can see us, so we have to watch what we do," I say. "You certainly are different." Bodies have their own morals. A woman so close and so intent on being seductive worries me. I am surprised by my body's response and suddenly alarmed by what Meriam will think. "Our drinks are waiting."

"Let's finish the dance," she whispers pleading. "Kiss me, I've never been kissed by an Arab. Up to now, my kisses are kosher." She glances at Sam.

"You're not funny," I say, but her lips find their way. I am being kissed.

"What's going on?"

But I know what's going on. Meriam sees it.. Sam sees it. I wonder what Meriam's thinking.

Goddamn.

Meriam's face grows acid pale.

I jerk my mouth away from Janice. "Lady, we're going back to the bar." I lead her off the floor, furious. I feel like a worm has crawled into my bones and eaten my soul. I don't know what feels worse, the stupidity or the dishonesty.

Janice yields to my stern voice and walks sheepishly beside me. I will deposit her and leave. We find Bill looking pathetic and almost drunk.

"What's going on?" Janice asks me. "First, you screw up my reservation, then you embarrass me on the dance floor."

Her arm is still in mine. "Lady," I say, "I only met you and your partner 15 minutes ago."

"This is my drunken brother," she says. I glance back looking for Meriam, but I don't find her.

Judy, the hostess, comes to say, "Your table is ready."

"My table is the one down there," Janice raises her voice, pointing to where Riyad and Esther are sitting. "You can tell Sam that Janice is here, if he hasn't seen me yet. I don't want to stay for dinner. Order me a cab."

People around look at me with tolerant smiles.

"Help me carry this slob, will you. He's been drinking since noon."

"Okay," I say. I remember Mother saying, "If a cup of fine china is cracked, nothing can fix it. The only thing left is to pick up the pieces."

"What's eating you?" Janice attacks. "I'm the one who got hurt and you're acting like the victim. Do Arabs always act like this?"

I feel the blood rushing to my eyes. I would like to slap her, but I don't.

"Hello, Janice," Sam calls from behind me. "I'll take over, Sameer."

"Hi, doll," Janice says. "Why don't you introduce me to the rest of the family?"

"The rest of the family is not here, and you're leaving right now," Sam says sternly.

I stand puzzled. Janice puts her arm around a staggering Bill and drags him with her. "Let's get out of this joint. We're not wanted."

"We better get back," Sam says.

"Where's Meriam?" I blurt out.

"She went home." Sam doesn't elaborate, and we walk together to the table.

"I hope Meriam will feel better," Riyad tells Sam.

Sam assures him she will be okay and sits by Esther.

I go to the kitchen. At the grill I take a knife to cut a tomato. The knife is shaking in my hand.

"What's going on, Sameer?" a baffled Judy asks me. "I've never seen you like this."

A flash of guilt twists inside me. How can I face Meriam, explain my behavior in front of her husband's mistress?

Sam walks into the kitchen cheerfully. "You saved my skin."

I ponder Sam's notion of "saving skins." Did I lose mine in the process?

"Adultery's becoming tiresome," Sam whispers to me in one of his trips to the kitchen. "In a country where there's an AA for everything, it's amazing there isn't a BA - - Betrayal Anonymous. Maybe I should organize one." He leaves before I can reply.

I work past midnight. Riyad and Esther love the food. Esther is in a devouring mood. Riyad wants to see me tomorrow. Urgent.

I call Meriam, hoping some sensible apology will come to mind. The phone rings forever. Judy watches.

I feel I am sinking in a swamp of my creation, chopping parsley and living with Meriam in hiding while politicians are savagely destroying my people in refugee camps.

When Judy invites me for a cup of tea after work, I accept, trying to delay going home.

Judy lives in a three-decker in East Cambridge. She leads the way through a back stairway. She tiptoes ahead of me, her legs light and excited.

"Thomas is asleep," she says as she turns the key.

"Thomas?" I ask, entering the living room. Figures of saints and religious sentiments adorn the walls.

"Thomas is my twelve year old. He's a sound sleeper."

Judy fixes tea. I add lots of sugar, forever trying to recapture a sensation of sweet warmth from childhood.

"You looked worried tonight, Sameer. I prayed for you."

Judy is built wide and large. Her eyes are brown and quiver with a supportive smile.

"Thanks for your prayers, but tonight prayers won't bring me salvation."

"I watched you with that evil woman. I was worried about you. She was full of sin and lust."

"So was I."

"I don't believe that." She takes off her sweater. Her blouse is buttoned up to the neck. I notice her broad chest, broad wrists, broad ankles. I'm ready to tell her about Meriam, but the angels in the background on the wall have a glazed look that prevents me.

I think you're a nice man. You deserve a different kind of woman."

"She's not my girl."

"I know. She's Sam's."

"You know?"

"Everybody does. Sometimes there are two or three of them."

Blessed be Mary, who kept her innocence until the very last moment.

"I pray for Sam, too," Judy says. "He doesn't try to pick up waitresses. You have to give him credit for that."

"How do you know?"

"He jokes about it, but I don't think he wants you to know."

"Why not?"

"Because you live with them. I like his wife - - she has real class. The waitresses gossip that she's kind of cold."

I resist the temptation to tell her Meriam is full of tropical passion. Instead, I ask Judy about her husband.

"I don't have one."

"I mean your ex."

"I never had one. Are you shocked?" Her eyes brighten.

"I am."

"I used to be a different kind of woman, different language, different dress." She straightens her skirt on her knees. "Thomas doesn't have a father, but there is a Father who cares for all of us, including you."

I try to imagine Judy in a bikini with a sexually aggressive look, pulling a man to bed in a hailstorm of embarrassing words. I smile. "Hard to believe," I say.

"I don't lie, Sameer." She touches my hand for emphasis. "I was a lost woman until I found Jesus. I've been meaning to talk to you about the Lord ever since your father died, but you're always busy or in a rush.

Jesus helped me through my difficult times."

"You know I'm from Nazareth." I invoke my town as a shield against any attempt to save me.

"It's hard to believe you lived where Jesus did."

Nazareth is dusty now. Dry leaves in deathly color sift in the cold wind. Donkeys struggle under heavy loads in and out of the market. Smells are everywhere.

Judy interrupts my thoughts, "You'll like Thomas, he's a loving kid."

"Tell me about him." I lean back in my chair, hoping she'll talk more about Thomas and less about Christ.

"My mother left me with my grandparents and moved out of state."

"You never forgave her?"

"God is forgiving. I became attached to my grandparents, especially my grandfather, an Irishman who said whatever was on his mind. But Grandpa died when I was twelve. Things got worse after that. I dropped out of school. I smoked dope, sinned with many men, and hell followed."

The couch feels comfortable after a long day. Even the brass "Jesus Saves" sign flickers with acceptance on the wall. Judy's voice is monotonous. I slip into sleep. Judy's hands, covering me with a blanket, stir me awake.

"Goodnight," she says kissing me gently on the forehead.

"I'm not an icon." I draw her to me.

"No, Sameer, not yet," but she responds to my hug, and after a long kiss says, "I often wondered how your lips feel."

I forget about the twelve year old and draw her under the blanket. The more I draw her to me, the less she resists. All the "Jesus Saves" signs blaze around us.

"Not here, Sameer. Let's go to my room."

It feels colder in her room, with revival posters and ceramic crosses.

I hold her close, her bare body tight to mine. In the dim light I see a picture of her son staring at me, large round eyes and solemn mouth.

After an embarrassing period of frustration Judy says, "It's okay, Sameer. Maybe it's better this way."

I don't know what happened. I don't know whether I should apologize for trying to make love to her, or for not being able to. "I'm sorry. It's not my day."

We dress quickly and move back to the couch in the living room. Judy continues to talk about sin and salvation. She talks of a hill in Belmont where she goes to speak with God and sing prayers.

"Why don't you sing me some of those prayers."

"You're troubled, Sameer." Sitting with her legs tucked under, skirt pulled over, arm around my neck, and her clean bra now firmly in control of her hidden breasts, she begins singing in a coarse voice,

> I was guilty with nothing to say,
>
> And they were coming to take me away,
>
> But then a voice from Heaven was heard,
>
> That said let him go and take me instead.

A thin boy with ruffled hair comes to the door rubbing his eyes. "What time is it?" he asks in a sleepy voice.

"Sorry we woke you, honey. This is Mr. Sameer. I told you about him. He comes from the Holy Land."

Thomas mutters a faint, "Hi."

"Let me tuck you in." Judy gets up and hugs him away.

I'm ready to leave when she comes back. "Can you have Thanksgiving with us? You'd like Thomas," she says.

"Thanks, I'm not sure," I say, and leave as fast as I can.

The drive to Newton is fast. Even Watertown Circle is deserted at three in the morning. Sam and Meriam's spacious home stands dark and foreign among the trees. I enter quickly like a night prowler. My Hippie Christ murmurs, "How could you stand those glazed angels?" On my pillow I find a sealed envelope with my name on it. I recognize Meriam's green ink. My heart sinks in embarrassment. Meriam saw me with Janice, and I'm still chilled from my encounter with Judy.

I take Meriam's letter and hold it. Guesses scramble about the contents, her pain, my infidelity. I tear open the envelope.

"My Dearest Sameer," she writes. "I apologize for leaving so abruptly. I know more about Sam's mistresses than I admitted. I was furious about what Sam did. I felt it would be better if I left, certainly less explosive." The letter ends with, "Can I see you tomorrow? I promise you chilled wine and a warm body."

I know I can't stay with Sam and Meriam. Either I quit the husband or abandon the wife.

I don't deserve this letter. My fears vanish. I sink into bed thinking of the evening with Judy. "Mary, Mother of Jesus," I sigh. I ran to the wilderness and sinned on the way.

The guilt of unaccomplished sex weighs on me more than an accomplished act would. I fall asleep with the sound of Judy excitedly chanting and asking me to pray with her before sex, and the blurring sweet look of her son filling me with embarrassing irritation.

CHAPTER 19

Riyad looks at me puzzled. It's eleven a.m. I'm still dozing and unshaved. This morning it's difficult to face myself. Nightmares raged in my sleep, refusing to subside.

Riyad is excited about the night before, with Esther. "I had to tell Esther you were married before. She thought you were still a virgin. Can you believe it?"

"You must be kidding," I try to interrupt Riyad.

"She even told Meriam to fix you up with a nice Jewish girl. That was before that gorgeous piece paraded around you last night. I had to resist telling them stories about the Don Juan of Nazareth, about Suhailah, and others before Christine."

In one sweep Riyad stirs up memories I've spent ten years burying. In Nazareth, loss of virginity is destruction, shame. I was harassed by a puritan conscience. Floods of tears, a woman entreating. Tears of passion that erupt from shattered spines, not flattering tears.

My face twists to the past and freezes in horror on a pillar of salt. Gomorrah! The track of betrayals meanders all the way back to the first woman. I've prayed for those layers of mud and dirt to settle.

Riyad sees me as a man with a record to be proud of. I peek inside those memories to a cave of horrors.

"Now we can start double dating," Riyad says grinning. "Just like Americans, wear T-shirts, go to movies and eat popcorn. As a matter of fact, I miss Nazareth's pumpkin seeds. Huge mountains of salted seeds, home roasted. We used to eat them at the movies. How do you like American women?"

"I divorced the only one I knew intimately. I was faithful to her," I say, answering my own thoughts.

"I'll only marry an Arab, preferably one from Nazareth."

"Somebody like Esther?" I ask, testing.

"Esther? Oh, no. Esther is only," a sensuous smile covers his mouth and cheeks, "Mmm, Mmm."

I used to find Riyad's black and white perception of life quite attractive. There was a security in seeing life in bold colors. But hearing it now alarms me.

Riyad lights a cigarette and puffs smoke rings. "A woman of your own kind understands you, your smallest sighs and smiles." He pulls a chair to the window and looks outside, then turns abruptly.

"Our friend from Nazareth, Fuad, called yesterday. He just returned from home. He had a message from your mother, one she didn't want to pass through the Israeli censors. She wants to sell your property and come here. Especially since you're divorced. Your brother is happily married at home. Conditions there are worse than ever. The Israeli army is brutal. They shoot demonstrators in the West Bank, kill children, women, everybody."

"Sell our land?" I repeat in disbelief.

Riyad's face tightens. "She shouldn't sell. None of us should sell what little is left of our land. We can't have a homeland, have a Palestine, without land."

I was born at home. Grandmother and Father died at home. Our land is close to the Church of Annunciation where Mary knew of her divine fertility. God and blood are mixed in our land. Without our land I'd be orphaned. Mother knows very little English, she'd have a cruel exile here. She'll be homesick the rest of her days. I know what she'd say, "I'm happy where my son lives, I'm happy if he's happy." And she'd mean it. Love always came easy to her.

Through the window the trees are bare. Newton's houses look firmly based, settled. Riyad and I are out of place in the heart of Newton.

"I can't wait to finish school and start working," Riyad murmurs. Looking at me closely he says, "I think you're wasting your energy talking to Zionist organizations. The most you get are the patient ears of one liberal Jew. You won't convert them to our cause. It's misplaced energy." He crushes the butt of his cigarette in the ashtray.

"Are you doing any better?" I'm on the defensive.

"We should talk to Arab Americans and to non-Jews. We should enlist their support."

"I thought you were trying to convert Sam, not me."

"Sam wants to visit refugee camps in Lebanon and see the 'true face of Zionism.'"

"That's news to me. Sam is not fanatic, but he certainly is a hardcore Zionist."

"He's liberal enough about Esther and me."

"And Esther?"

"She knows my politics and she's transferring to Brandeis."

"Really?" I try to hide my pleasure at the news of her living in Waltham. "A jug of Carmel wine, loaf of Jewish challah, and Esther," I kid Riyad.

"I'm transferring too, next semester," he continues. "I've been accepted at Harvard."

"Congratulations." I slap his back.

"I was thinking we might rent an apartment together," Riyad continues quietly.

"Done." Riyad offers my solution.

CHAPTER 20

I am lying in bed thinking. Making love to Meriam has washed away my feelings of inadequacy with Judy. I am engulfed by a peaceful silence.

"Sameer, talk to me." Meriam touches my lips gently with her fingers.

"So you know more about Sam's mistresses?"

"Sarah, Sally, Barb, Janice—tell me when to stop." Meriam laughs nervously, moving her body close to mine. "I know more than I admitted. I never minded before. And it sounds absurd that I should mind now, when I have you. But I do. Sam claims it's only lust and essential for his survival."

"How come you didn't mind before?"

"I guess I thought maybe I wasn't satisfying Sam. I don't believe love between two people changes just because one of them goes to bed with someone else. Intellectually I don't believe it." Meriam covers herself with the sheet up to her neck. She can never be nude and serious at the same time. I move to kiss her, but I sense she would like to talk.

"I feel more and more, lately, that my education is wasted. I'm trapped. I used to feel guilty for lack of guilt, now I'm guilty and very tense."

I haven't seen this part of Meriam before. "Does Sam know this?"

"Sam and I live in two different worlds."

"You relate to each other so well, you're so nice together. You're discreet."

"Sam's attentive, if that's what you mean. You see it. He serves me first, opens the door, gets me flowers, keeps his famous temper in check. But he doesn't hear my screams, my loneliness, my pain."

"You're affectionate together," I say. "I've witnessed many hugs."

"We care about each other. I care about him. We care like human beings who live together should, but he's totally incapable of sensing my emotions. I'm afraid I'm equally incapable of feeling his. It pains me. We live in two remote districts - - like in a confederation." She stops and asks me to pour her some cognac. "With you it's different. You're right here inside me." She takes a sip of her drink. "Of course, we look happily married to everybody. Didn't you think so? And don't misunderstand - - compared to most of my friends, our marriage has solid foundations. Am I entitled to ask for more? Can we ask for more in life?"

"Miri, you have everything we're seeking. The United States, a country, a flag, wealth. Your world is as solid as this earth can offer in a lifetime. Compare that to a refugee camp - - or to my mother who has to sell our land. It's all so absurd."

"Sell the land?" Meriam, alert to my feelings, rushes to my hurt. "Why?"

"She wants to sell, then emigrate. She's afraid my brother will end up shot in a demonstration. When the life of a son is at stake, political arguments about keeping the land become a double-edged sword."

Meriam moves towards me and kisses my lips, my cheeks, and stays close to me. Her moist eyes give way to tears. I'm sorry Sameer," she says, "so sorry."

CHAPTER 21

"With a real goy in residence, we can at last justify a Christmas tree."
Sam stretches his arms, recycling his endless vigor, visibly enjoying his
brunch with Meriam and me. Noticing that we all haven't been spending
much time together lately, he complains to Meriam. "Sameer works too
long and far too hard."

It's like each of us is anxious to please the other two. We circle in
pleasing attempts. Even Meriam hugs Sam a touch longer in front of
me.

Sam's right. I have tried to drown myself in work. When I was
a student I selected my classes in pursuit of myself - - philosophy,
psychology and writing. I always enjoyed being a student, watching the
stage with all the props set for ideas: the professor's pipe, the ruffled
cool look of academics, the idiosyncrasies that seep through their
performance, the totally remote world which they create of debates and
ideas, their escape into a unique language of theories and mental games,
the seductive fascination of the students. I feet drunk in mind and heart,
like when reading the diaries of Marcus Aurelius and the letters of Pliny,
and realized that anguish has been central to human experience for the
last two thousand years.

Christmas with Sam and Meriam is bringing us back together. We
plan to cut our own tree. Meriam doesn't want a perfectly shaped one.
She wants a different kind of tree.

"We can pluck its bottom branches and leave a bushy top. Nothing
is symmetrical in human nature," I assure.

We find a tree, in Newton Center, with an odd branch stretching out
two feet in deformed imbalance. When the owner sees it, he chuckles
and tells us, "It's free. Christmas spirit."

"What kind of angel shall we hang up?" Sam chuckles.

The three of us recover from the Janice incident around coffee, drinks and dinner. The exit of Esther renews our togetherness. She leaves us in a fanfare, pulling me to her with a hug, as if she's moving to Pakistan.

"Thanks, love, for being sweet to Esther," Sam caresses Meriam's hair. "I was ready to abdicate my responsibility."

"Riyad made life much easier," Meriam says.

"I'll give them another year. They're both explosive. Either they'll live together or they'll pull the sky down in a separation scene."

Back in my room, my Hippie Christ asks me, "What's all the fuss about Christmas?"

"You're becoming a cynic," I accuse him.

At the Oasis the next day, I see a shadow from the past, a resemblance, a memory, a woman. I feel good, but who is she? She sits close to the open kitchen watching me, her face sending many images. I can't place her.

Lunch on Monday fills the Oasis with the elderly. Elderly women, with tired faces, sharing each other's feelings and weekends, as if human experience continues to surprise them with the same son, daughter, husband, and neighbor. Elderly men talking about the weather, slowly and disconnected, as if it's all that happens and can possibly happen in the universe. As if the ultimate storm in life is a snowstorm or a heat wave.

Sam, in a rash of emotional extravagance, plans a party. "For all religions," he announces to me, "ethnic groups, and races. I'm inviting Vera, Martin, Esther and Riyad, and Nicole and her parents. I told Riyad to come in a bulletproof vest, he's going to need it!"

I'm not sure if Sam means because of his in-laws or his homosexual guests. Sam is still amused by Richard and John as parents. His humor comes like torrential rain, and clears just as fast.

"You know, Sameer, your stay with us has been great. Before you moved in, when Meriam and I were alone, we were sitting on the edge of a seesaw. If one was up, the other was down. But now with the three of us, we're able to keep a better balance."

"I'm never prepared for Sam's confidences. They are unpredictable and I'm partially scared of surges of honesty, of me weakening and telling him I love Meriam. Honesty is starting to frighten me. Every time the three of us sit together, we face two that we love.

"Janice was kidding me about you. She finds you attractive."

"You mean you still see her after that scandal?"

"That woman comes with lots of earthy delights." Sam pours himself a cup of coffee, spilling it on his hand. "Ouch." He laughs. "Listen, Sameer, I have my own Lovers Bill of Rights."

My throat dries in suspense. Is he aware of Meriam and me?

"It's a Bill of Rights for freshmen lovers," he continues, drying his hand. "Article One: Lovers are entitled to complete confidentiality. Article Two: Honesty destroys harmony." His eyebrows knot in pleasant concentration and he adds, "Meriam is my good luck charm, ever since we've been married. You know. You've seen us very closely. Sometimes I think you can see things we don't see ourselves."

I'm tempted to tell Sam about my plans for sharing an apartment with Riyad, but the timing seems wrong.

CHAPTER 22

Sam is arranging the glasses, putting the finishing touch on his bar, lime and lemon to the side.

Meriam asks, "Sameer, do you like my flower arrangement?"

Sam says, "It's beautiful. The vase and flowers are great."

Suddenly, Meriam looks at me, then at Sam with her warm eyes. "I don't want you to enshrine me. You can build a mausoleum after I die. I want to live now. I want to be loved now."

"But we love you now, don't we, Sameer?" Sam never responds to serious remarks on the spot. He puts his arm around Meriam, she rests her head on his shoulder, and extends her other arm to touch me. We're ready for the party.

Vera arrives ahead of Martin, loaded with pies and family gossip. "Nicole is acquiring Italian body language with Josie fussing over her all the time. Oh, and John is trying to become a folk singer."

Martin doesn't even know his way around the house, and asks me where the back door to the garden is. He seems reserved.

Sam, in a rare display of congeniality to his father-in-law, tries to engage Martin in conversation.

"How's business?"

"I'm not in business, Sammy, thank you," Martin replies, clearly allergic to any association between the academe and business.

I know how Sam cringes at being called Sammy.

"Can I get you a drink?"

"Let's try to have a conversation before we get drunk, Sammy."

Nicole, Richard and John arrive in a rush of restrained excitement. I help them get settled. I have missed Richard's dry wit and John's flair.

I see Riyad and Esther arriving. Afraid of embarrassing questions about Nicole's mother, I go out to the driveway and try to explain the situation to Riyad.

"The decadence of the Western world," he tells me in Arabic. Once inside, Riyad sits staring at the new family with total incomprehension.

Nicole, handed from one person to another, remains peaceful. It's hard to extract her from Meriam's arms.

"Oh, Nicole," Martin tries to take Nicole in arms against her will.

"It's obvious Martin never held a girl younger than a college freshman," Sam mutters through the corner of his mouth.

Riyad holds Nicole and she smiles. "You see, all JAPS love him," Sam says.

"Cut it out, Sam," Esther laughs.

I wonder if she's already in love.

Martin, giving up on Nicole, turns to his son. "Richard, I want to talk to you sometime. I'd like you to draw up a will for us."

Vera steps in. "Martin, honey, this is a holiday celebration."

"The topic scares her. There is no right time," Martin tells Meriam.

"It scares me too," Meriam replies.

Outsiders are a godsend in family tensions. They become ideal scapegoats. "Are you afraid to talk about death?" Martin shifts his attention to Riyad.

"We don't consider death a party topic if that's what you mean," Riyad says.

I feel the sharp edge of the conversation in my heart and think of my father's death. Women clad in black who follow the men, who follow the dead. Life is invoked. "Our consolation is in your survival," people would have told me. It's an ill omen to visit anybody, as if death is contagious. Mourning women, clad in black, refer to death as "the plague" and "the curse," ending their wailing with, "May God damn death."

Meriam calls us to dinner. Riyad is not aware that it's the Jewish Hanukkah celebration. Martin lights the candles and starts reading outloud.

Riyad, to my side, asks me, "What the hell is going on?"

"Rejoicing over a great victory—two thousand years ago."

"Why don't they get out of the West Bank and Golan Heights so that we can rejoice for a change?" Riyad mutters loudly.

Richard whispers to him, "They need a signal from God for an exit like that."

"An effective signal from the White House will do the trick okay," Riyad says. "Ben Gurion pulled out of the Sinai Desert after a telephone call from Eisenhower."

"It's useless arguing with Riyad," Esther says apologetically.

"For us, its not an esoteric argument," Riyad says, becoming the center of attention. "You seem to grasp the importance of it for your people in Egypt two thousand years ago, but are totally blind about its relevance to us. We locked our doors, took our keys and fled from your armies. The French could go back to France, the Germans to Germany, but not us."

"You realize the Middle East could cause a global war," Martin says.

"The great powers can blow each other out of existence," Riyad says with a sarcastic smile. "We can survive in desert conditions, can't we, Sameer?"

I'm amused by the image of Riyad surviving in a desert. In Nazareth, Riyad lives in a large house, high ceilings, marble pillars, and endless rooms and corridors. Certainly not in a tent.

"Have you heard of Nazi concentration camps?" Martin asks.

"Why should we pay for the crimes committed by Nazis, Germans, Poles and others? Frankly, you won't get a tear from me. My tears have dried over the refugees and the tragedies you continue to inflict on us, inside Israel and outside it."

Obviously concerned that Riyad will lose his temper further, Esther bends over him and puts her arms around him. "Darling, what do I inflict on you?" And like a circus hypnotist, she's quickly able to thrust her hands between the lion's jaws.

Riyad smiles calmly. Esther and Riyad, women and men. But then I look at John and Richard - - man and man.

"We are going to win," Riyad says. "Besides, we could do it together. We did in the past."

"Sameer, you're quiet," Vera wants to diffuse the lightening.

My hatred has been corroded by liberal views. I have seen the movies on concentration camps. I could never comprehend how it happened. My hatred has been blunted by humanitarian, civil libertarian views. I don't talk about this. Meriam and Sam, the three of us have transcended the argument. Transcended? Or are we numb?

"Why don't you live and let live?" Martin packs his pipe, getting ready for a prolonged argument.

"You advocate live and let live when it serves your interest. The strong tell it to the weak. It smacks of Western culture and false naïveté." Riyad is always ready.

"Live and let live?" Richard turns to his father. "You can't have it within families, yet alone nations."

"You," Sam points his finger at Martin, "can start by recognizing the rights of the Palestinians." Sam is mischievously stirring up trouble.

"What's this a masquerade in sheep's clothing, Sam old boy? Aren't you, or weren't you, enlisted in the Israeli army?" Martin asks.

"Oh, I'm just a welcome wagon committee for Israeli officers who visit the U.S. Those who don't know English well enough to find their way around. Just for extra money. You know the expensive tastes of your daughter."

I remember Sam hosted such a group when I went with Meriam to visit Vera and Martin. Sam stands to get more drinks. I go to assist him.

"Holy Moses," Sam tells me, "isn't this quite a mix. Martin is baiting

Riyad on all his favorite topics. And aren't Richard and his playmate quite a sight?"

We take the drinks back. Vera disapproves of Martin drinking. "I'll have to drive back," she says, her thin lips tightly closed and twisted like the buckle of a woman's purse.

Undeterred, Martin engages Riyad about his American experience.

"I can already see the collapse in the educational system." Martin nods his head emphatically.

"The schools here are a mystery to me," Riyad says. "I see kids coming in and out of school, but I never see books. Remember, Sameer, how we used to get new books from the school every year and hold onto them with pride as a sign of education?"

I do. The fresh smell of new books and excitement over the year of learning ahead. And, if there were novels, we would read all of them in the first week.

"All they need," Martin says, "is a chip and a computer. The soul is evaporating in the arcades of education. I grant you this point, Riyad. I agree with you on the decadence of the West."

"But, honey, the people around you are not decadent," Vera interrupts.

"We have a mood of…" Martin searches for a word, "disposability. Yes, disposability in this country of short dreams and quick desires."

"It's a much better country than it was. Our parents, they lived a hard life." Vera is clearly tense about the direction Martin is taking.

"This is not a society, this is an animal farm, a feeding lot. This is a pet shop gone wild. We live in glass cages, alone, like single pythons in pet shops, forever waiting to strike." Martin abruptly ends the conversation and becomes silent.

"Martin is angry. There was a horrible mugging and rape on his campus last week," Vera explains to Riyad.

Anxious to break the tension I suggest that John play the guitar.

John plays and sings simple tales. Love lost, the polluted earth, wars won and lost, nostalgia for a different world, an innocent world.

Much later, after everybody leaves, the house stays charged with pockets of feelings - - where Vera sat, her napkin folded tightly, where Martin left his ashes, where Riyad sat staring at the family, where Richard and John sat resigned. Cleaning the house does not rid it of tension. The pockets linger for a long time after their departure.

CHAPTER 23

Winter plunges us into discussions of winter. We live between snowstorms, anticipating snowstorms, and nature becomes the scapegoat for man's frustration with man. In the center of it, we forget that spring ever existed, and memories of heat waves are gone.

One day Sam returns home unexpectedly. Only luck saves us and I decide to move out. I have a strong premonition, fate has a different deck of cards for me.

I go apartment hunting with Riyad - - I ask him not to mention that I'll be moving. I'd like to select the right moment to tell Meriam. My right moments have a chronic tendency to arrive late.

Sam gives Riyad a lot of addresses for apartments. While climbing endless staircases and entering many cramped rooms, I think about the consequences. I'll be leaving Meriam and the incredible comfort of the house in Newton.

Finally, we stumble into a side street address in Watertown where furniture is being loaded into a moving truck. "That's going to be our place," Riyad says.

A Sicilian lady invites us in, in broken English, serves us coffee and brandy, and takes our deposit.

We rent the top floor. Our apartment has many rooms, four or five, with balconies overlooking neighbor's bedrooms. The people moving out, a young couple, eye us like intruders.

We rent the top floor. Angela, the Sicilian lady, and her three daughters and two sons live on the first floor. We do not meet her husband.

"He speaks no English," Angela says smiling, and we assume he is at work. "They are good neighbors here, Italians," Angela announces. "Many are my friends and one Irish family. Good people."

"Do you own this apartment?"

"Me, no," she waves her hand in utter astonishment. "A Jew with lots of money owns it."

"It seems we can't avoid them. We're stuck with them here too." Riyad laughs cynically. Esther must be on his mind.

"Mina Al Jimal ila Aljimal," I say, reciting a poem about an Arab who emigrated from Syria. Out of curiosity he found himself lining up with Americans in front of a tent, and paid his last penny to see a camel inside. He wrote, "From camels and back to camels!"

We take the address of the real estate agent from Angela and leave feeling relieved. We go to the realtor to sign the lease.

"In America you see everything," Riyad exclaims on the way. "Did you see all those saints and shrines in Angela's living room and that furniture? She is still in Sicily."

"It's not the same for her," I say. "In Sicily that lady wouldn't have an accent. That's a hell of a difference."

"But we would," Riyad answers laughing.

I plan a long-winded, thank you speech about my impending exit. Sam, instead, takes me by surprise. Are you planning to move in with Riyad?"

"Yes."

"If you're doing this because of Esther, you don't have to. Esther will be happier if you stay in her room here and she moves in with Riyad!" Sam's humor strips my words of their impending seriousness.

"I don't think I'll be able to say thank you in the right way."

"Please don't because you're going to see more of us in Watertown." Sam puts his arm around Meriam.

They start talking about the move, about plants I should take with me, furniture they can't use, kitchen utensils. Meriam moves in to fill the emptiness of the new apartment. Instead of an emotionally charged encounter, Meriam ends up driving toward Watertown to check and decorate.

When Meriam's white Continental pulls up in front of the apartment, it attracts the attention of kids and neighbors. Meriam steps out of it—elegant, energetic, and full of determination, with Sam and me trailing her.

"I've never been in the area and it's only 20 minutes away," she says.

Twenty minutes away to the other side of heaven. Am I already outside its gates?

I pack my belongings - - leaving my Hippie Christ until the end. Meriam, neatly stacking my books, looks at me suddenly.

"You never talk about Christine."

"No."

"Do you see her?"

"No."

"Do you think of her?"

"I used to."

"Is the sky clear now?" Meriam looks concerned.

"You are my spring," I tell her. "Christine seems like a distant storm."

"Spring is short."

For once I wish I had the insight of a fortune teller. Is our spring short?

"Sameer, you're not answering me."

I wish Mother was around to throw a bit of salt to protect against evil, or say a prayer against the evil eye, so that evil is washed away from me, from her family, from the house.

"What happens to lovers at the end? You're my first. I don't know." Meriam sounds anxious.

"They eventually die." The answer murmurs itself though me.

"What?" she asks surprised. "It's becoming scary to talk to you about love. Sometimes I can't read you."

"Try reading me from right to left. That's my natural order," I say, hoping to defuse the gloom. "I'm sorry. I don't know what hit me." I shake my head trying to dispel a haunting mood, a mysterious spasm.

"I am going to read you from right to left. You are going to teach me Arabic. But, please Sameer, let's stop this. Let me take you for a drive."

"Have I scared you? Do I look that bad?"

"No," she says smiling.

We get as far as Cleveland Circle, a very busy and strange convergence of traffic. Restless cars are edging us forward, as if in a boat that lost its oars. A car honks impatiently behind, and we finally roll out of the jam toward the more sedate parts of Newton. Meriam is quiet.

She drives past the high school. I can hear the sighs of boredom coming out of the building. She is driving with determination in a direction I don't recognize. Finally she stops on the highway by a cemetery.

The cemetery is huge, its graves spilling down to the edge of the pavement. Death is catching up with the living. The headstones are polished and shining like shoes of pallbearers.

"Is this our destination?" I ask her puzzled.

"Yes," she says with a great grin, pulling the car even closer to the granite monuments.

The cemetery is winter dry except for some snow patches, all its tears frozen.

She puts her soft hand on my lips. "Wait," she whispers. "When I'm depressed, I come here for shock therapy. Sam would say this is the bottom line. Where shall we go from here?"

We smile affectionately and embrace. Love speaks eloquently at doorsteps of cemeteries.

Returning home, we pass again by the high school. The boredom that wraps school buildings is livelier than the stillness of the cemetery we just left.

"Ana bahibbik. First lesson in Arabic," I say.

"I love you too."

CHAPTER 24

The day I move to Watertown, Meriam at my side, Esther and Riyad at the receiving end - - there are no goodbyes. I hang my Hippie Christ facing my bed. The first night I stay there his eyes, sorrowful and filled with irony, tell me, "Sleep, for the night is short."

Is it self-indulgence to say I'm surprised I can sleep at all? For me, peaceful sleep happens only in Nazareth on a straw mat in the shade of our mulberry tree, with spots of sun dancing around the leaves, the birds. I'm looking into space, the scents of summer strong and dizzying. Youth has so much time to waste, so much free time. With a sudden burst of energy, I'd stand and play with sticks or imaginary drums, or become absorbed in the movement of a bee. Nazareth is a bond between the earth and me.

In Watertown, I surprise myself and sleep soundly.

The apartment is starting to acquire Riyad's distinct flavors, the aroma of allspice, cardamom, nutmeg and cinnamon. Water pipes, camels, hand carved from olive trees, and a huge library of novels and poetry in Arabic spreads out on the floor and window sills. The Palestinian flag and map are displayed in the dining room. With our first drink, Riyad toasts an Independent Palestine.

Esther almost chokes on her drink and Sam says, "Your place looks like a Zionist nightmare." Laughter dulls the political edge.

The apartment in Watertown is becoming an escape, back to the roots. Palestinians gather in our living room. We throw mats and pillows around in anticipation of long evenings and serious discussions. Instead, we end up listening to nostalgic music about the village fountains where lovers meet. Soon I realize that time I spend with Riyad is time I don't spend with Meriam.

Riyad agrees with me about Mother. With no friends here and not knowing English, it would be tragic for my mother to immigrate. So

I write her a painful letter. I write that it will be hard for her without friends, that people here don't have time for conversation, not in the bank, nor the grocery store, nor the street. What would she do here? Watch television all day long waiting for us to return at night. How little do I know the heart of Mother. The loneliness of no language will be too cold to bear. Where time is of the essence, there is no patience for sign language.

The first time Esther shows up at a party for our friends, hanging on Riyad's arm in tight sweater and jeans, his face turns colors. Riyad is becoming embarrassed about his sex life, and Esther is unwilling to settle for his bedroom alone.

"What the hell is going on?" Esther corners me. "I don't give a damn if he's Palestinian. Why does he get so uptight about me with his Arab friends?" Her breath wraps me in mist of wine.

"I blame history."

"Hell, Sameer, if you think history doesn't reach our bedroom, you're mistaken." Her face brightens as she imitates Riyad, "'The Palestinians shall overcome.' Riyad says that at the most untimely moments, and, of course, with a broad grin and laughing. Can you believe I put up with that?"

"Why are you telling me all of this?"

"I'm lonely, Sameer - - lonely, lonely, lonely. Do you know what I wrote this morning?" Esther shows me a crumpled paper. "Here, read it."

I take it from her with reluctance and read: "I'm in arid loneliness, I feel life is a dry well, its walls cracking for a drop of love. A desolate grave that doesn't get flowers even on Memorial Day, not even one lousy plastic rose."

"You shouldn't feel this way," I tell her, trying to touch her shoulder. "What about all the love you get from Sam, from everybody?"

"Nobody gives a damn."

"What about all your causes and movements. Peace, war, Israel and all the rest?"

"Scared of having free time. That's all," she says with courage, her eyes starting to tear. "I'd exchange it all for one sincere 'I love you.' Maybe I should join the Moonies, Born Again Christians, or Buddhists where they say 'I love you' all the time." She smiles in tears. "Riyad doesn't love me, but even his political hatred has more human passion than I find in most guys."

"You're a fool, Esther. Love is just a matter of perception. Stretch in a different direction and you'll see it differently."

"For God's sake, Sameer, you're an incurable Mr. Feeling Wonderful. Where do you see love in my life today? Right now?"

"I hate to sound like a tape on positive thinking, but life is not meant to be a funeral. Get married, have children, and love them."

"Just like Sam loves my mother and my mother loves me? And you love your ex, I suppose." Biting is an instinct with Esther, I don't think she can help it.

"But Sam - - he loves you," I say with confidence.

"Yes, Sam loves me okay, in between screwing women and when Meriam is not watching." Esther flushes with anger. "I love Riyad. It's crazy. Everybody tells me, 'With so many nice Jewish boys at Brandeis, why the hell a Palestinian?'" Her laughter dies abruptly. "You seem to manage well with Dad and Meriam. Politics are not in your way."

Caught in the firing line, I mumble. "Well, of course, Sam and Meriam are unusual friends." Until now, I thought Ester existed in a zone of self-confidence. To see her stripped of all that is painful. "I don't know what to tell you," I add. "I just came out of such a mood myself."

"Never mind." Esther reaches over, kisses me on the cheek, friendly and grateful. Recovering her usual mischief, she asks, "Why was Riyad born an Arab?"

"Why were you born Jewish?"

CHAPTER 25

I'm the only one left with Sam at the Oasis, it's very late. A flashing ambulance out the window attracts our attention. We've just closed the Oasis and are sitting down for a nightcap. Ever since I moved from the house Sam delays me after hours for a drink. We walk outside to watch the ambulance. Two elderly men are standing on a porch looking apprehensive while two women rush in, then out, with a man on a stretcher.

Will this man ever return? I wonder. Did my father open his eyes in the last stretch? Abba lama shabaqtani - - Father, why have you abandoned me?

"I know sex will do me in one day," Sam tells me smiling pointing to the ambulance. He turns around and goes back inside. "I'm just like Riyad."

His comment about Riyad surprises me. "Sex, not love?" I say hoping to steer the discussion away from Riyad.

"Pure sex. I love the whole process. A curl in the hair, a look, a sentence, a touch too long, motel rooms, the flood of illusions, delusions, heat, explosions." Sam stretches, tipping his chair backwards.

"I think Meriam is great," I say sounding like a carefully worded State Department bulletin.

"God, Sameer, none of them are important to me. Meriam's my real anchor. The rest keep me flying. If I was saddled with any of those women, I'd be completely wretched."

"I don't follow you. You just finished describing the anatomy of your orgies to me."

"Not exactly." Sam wipes the table impulsively. "After sex, a timer always ticks. 'Sam,' it says, 'get out. Out as fast as you can!' All of them want to know something about Meriam and me, my children, my age, my income, and you name it. If I don't rush out, they'd be extracting

SAM, MERIAM, AND ME

a wedding date! So, I try to escape right away, before the expected conversation suffocates my pleasure. One thing keeps happening - - I can't say no." Sam waves his arms helplessly. "When Janice called the next morning and said, 'Honey, I'm horney,' I forgot the scandal and my anger - - and asked her, 'When?'" He looks at me pensively. "You're the Oasis philosopher, you tell me. How come I go through this, time after time - - like a programmed computer?"

"You sound like you need a team of shrinks," I tell him, trying to laugh it off.

He gulps more cognac and ignores my comment. "I know their stock analysis. He is incapable of love, they'd say. Avenging an Oedipal problem. Utter nonsense. Give me the excitement of true love anytime." In typical fashion, Sam sums it all up, "What the hell," he says, and stops. You'll drive me home, won't you? I've been drinking."

In the car Sam rests on his elbow and sleeps.

His question keeps ringing in my mind. I have no answer either. Maybe the answer is buried deep, many thousand years back, in the bone marrow of our ancestors. Maybe the answer is meshed in human history. Maybe it's the same answer for Arabs and Jews.

CHAPTER 26

I stand to the side, skeptical of political tornados. Politics lead to mental paradise but rarely to earthly ones.

Riyad's involvement with Esther pulls him outside. We often meet at midnight. Sam is a frequent visitor at our Watertown apartment.

"I have to chaperon my daughter, especially with him," he says, and the three of them laugh heartily. The three of them operate in a strange unit, always emotionally charged, always in opposition. Between American, Israeli and Palestinian views, there is a lot to oppose.

Riyad is stretching on throw pillows, Esther purring lustfully in his arms, and Sam sipping Arak. The sound percolates in catacombs of the mind, with strange visions, under pressure of liquor. Riyad thinks he's showing Sam the light and Sam could help explain our dilemma to Americans.

Sam is pragmatic. Is peace becoming profitable? When I mention all this to Meriam, she is equally puzzled.

"What's the catch?" she asks.

Meriam wants me to teach her Arabic. Sam laughs at what is happening to his family - - Riyad is reforming his politics, and I'm Arabizing his wife. Arabic lessons are ineffective. The utmost we reach are the complex letters. Half the seduction is vision, and we spend most of our time wrapped in passion.

She says, "I'm incapable of speaking afterwards."

When Sam starts excusing himself, leaving us to our Arabic lessons, and going to join Esther and Riyad in Watertown, I wonder. No, I don't wonder anymore. I'm afraid to ask myself, "Does everybody see?"

CHAPTER 27

One morning without any warning, Riyad tells me, "If Meriam was my wife, I'd kill her. Don't get excited," he interrupts. "I like her, she is gentle, she has class, she is sympathetic to us - - but if my wife screwed around, I'd kill her."

Riyad must have noticed that we spent a lot of time behind locked doors. "Between us there is more than screwing around," I tell him, anger gushing into my face.

"You sound like a teenager, Sameer. What ties man and woman is sex. Straight, crude, and beautiful sex. The rest depends on your tinted lenses."

"Meriam is past being a sex object." Even in my own ears, I sound like a second-rate woman's lib documentary.

"She's using you. She has the best of both worlds - - comfort from Sam and romance from you."

"Riyad, when I left Christine, I was numb, deaf, and blind from the shock. Meriam brought me back to my senses."

"It's departure from your senses. She's married. She's Sam's wife." Riyad doesn't mince words.

"What about Sam's daughter?" I say.

"She knows where she stands. We'll never get married."

"Of course, I know Meriam is married. There is no way around that. I wrestle with that all the time. I can't explain it logically. If I was living in a different age or culture, maybe I wouldn't be facing this. There are many things in life I wrestle with, but can't change or explain."

"So, do something about it."

"Life rests with no answers. I'm not sure logic or morals can explain life, mine or anybody's."

Riyad draws deeply on his cigarette. "So much is happening to us."

142

"I know. We're changing."

"Oh, the hell with it," Riyad says and stands up to pour himself a glass of Arak. He looks me straight in the eyes. "What's happening to you, Sameer?"

"Nothing," I sigh.

"You sound like an educated Roman slave."

"What the hell do you mean?"

"You fell in love with your slave owner," Riyad says grinning.

"Your metaphor stinks," I tell him and leave for the Oasis.

All the way to work I debate with myself whether Riyad is right. Is distance rinsing off our authentic faces? Are we growing new, deformed ones in our Diaspora? One lemon tree in our garden, in Nazareth, sometimes bears a lemon that's shaped abnormally with stretched edges and aberrations. "Ajabeh," we call it, deformity. I have acquired such a face, and somehow I feel I'd like to peel it off.

That evening my Hippie Christ whispers in my dreams, "Both Roman slaves and slave owners are in ruins today."

My concern about Sam's suspicion is dwindling. I feel like a medieval monk attending to the smallest details. I worry that my meetings with Meriam are becoming mellow. The less love, the more anxiety.

"What are your plans for the future?" Meriam asks me one day.

"No plans. It's difficult to have plans these days."

"Do you really intend to continue as a cook?"

"I enjoy it. It's good pay."

"What about all the rest, Sameer?"

Nazareth. I drift back. At thirteen, Riyad asks me, "What do you want to become?"

"A writer," I say, "And you, Riyad?"

"A political leader - - no, a military leader." Riyad has been going straight in that direction.

"What about writing?" Meriam revives the question.

"A dream. Like all the rest of my past, it glitters in a tear."

Meriam is barefoot and the bare floor of my bedroom in Watertown makes her look more naked, her slender toes more bare. I look closely at her. We've gone a long way on the path of familiarity. We have stripped and dressed each other. Meriam's mystique and the early tense excitement are replaced by a sense of ease- - of comfort. We are building a garden behind steel walls.

"Do you miss me sometimes?" I ask her, a question asked by lovers through the centuries, seeking confirmation.

"I do, I do. I don't even go into your room in Newton, afraid to see the changes."

"It's lovely to be together." Clichés have recently been cropping in our conversation.

"You should tell me, Sameer, if you get tired of me. Maybe I'm being selfish having you to myself like this."

The mood of this conversation makes me feel uneasy. These exchanges sound like emotional fillers when there is nothing else to discuss.

At times, I simply brush off the absurdity of the situation and rationalize that my behavior is in line with abnormal surroundings. I find myself tilting my head to see if my life is balanced. Life is cracked, I start telling myself. When I see harmony between a tender couple or a loving mother and her child, I am embarrassed about the elaborate system of self-deceit I have already grown in my hybrid mind.

In Nazareth, I could hear the voice of Mother asking, "My son, my dear son, is this the best we brought you up to do?" But I hear a different voice from father. "You're breaking the heart of your Mother. Sameer, act like a man." And a man to him is all that is honorable and decent.

CHAPTER 28

Amazing how houses take the shape of their tenants - - a few more water pipes and worry-beads around and it would look like home in Nazareth. Riyad stretches, trying to touch the ceiling. "I'm reading the Boston Globe, filled with apprehension about the Middle East. Riyad stops in the middle of a stretch to look at the headline.

"Rubbish news," Riyad says with his usual confidence. "And you're a pacifist. You should join the Dalai Lama and meditate in order to change the world. We have to fight dirty. Nothing is illegal for survival. Grassroots. That's the answer."

"Grassroots. What the hell is that, and how do you intend to do it, skinhead style? Like a haircut."

"Something like that. It is the only panacea. I'm even going to write my dissertation on it," Riyad says smiling.

"A treatise on brutal imagination?"

"Since when are you a cynic?" Riyad is surprised.

"Allow me to express a 'cook's' position on the topic."

"Cut the crap, Sameer. Go 'cook it' around Americans. Why do you hide in the Oasis?"

"It doesn't always lead to progress," I say, ignoring his comment.

"It damn well should. Liberal humanists like you weaken determination."

"I read somewhere that Stalin poisoned Gorky," I say, "Gorky must have thrown up over his revolutionary ideals on his death bed."

"Drinking Arabic coffee, listening to Arabic music, and cooking Arabic food doesn't change things," he screams. Riyad leaves me abruptly to join Sam and Esther.

Riyad is proud of the magic effect his fingers leave wherever they touch, a toxic mixture of self-deception. I wonder where Esther is in all of this?

Should I feel insulted that Sam, Esther and Riyad have no place for my marginal introspection? I'm busy with Meriam and the normal layers of emotional fog that sweep early in waking hours and extend until my sleep.

At night, I have a nightmare. I see the white teeth of politicians smiling over gullible crowds, delivering rhetoric and venom, their gold filled cavities flashing over fleeing families and dead bodies.

Spring is coming. It's been a long winter.

CHAPTER 29

Meriam is enjoying the sun in the back yard. Early spring has left a transparent tan on her body. She is in a pretty turquoise bathing suit, thin stripes, low cut on the front, high cut on the sides. I put my arms around her and feel the full sensuality of spring in her hug.

The political arguments with Riyad are bothering me. I'm afraid I'll wake up one day and feel like a White Russian, his dream of retrieving his country dying out like a cigarette butt discarded by a negligent driver.

"I feel helpless," I say. "I'm running in small circles around you, around my work, and Riyad."

She is startled. "What is this, the age of despair?" She takes my hand and rests it between her knees. "Do you still love me?"

"Despair is life without love, life without dreams. Sometimes I see myself without a country, without a language, with dreams about that mean so much to me and so little to others around me. Just a stray animal. Despair is a dead-end street, I fight it every day."

This conversation, like so many, ends up in the kitchen. Softly her lips, softly her breasts. When the despair of my soul unleashes and my mind is pale, my fingers seek her body for life. I bend feverishly on her, and we are left in sighs and whispers. When finally I'm inside her, it is a victory of pure sex, of sensuality over a limp soul.

Meriam opens her eyes. It's a fresh look of a woman just waking.

"Please stay by me," she entreats, "hold me." She holds me for the longest time close to her beating heart, her breasts pressed warmly between us. Suddenly I detect a tear from her cheek running on mine. I don't ask her why. Somehow her tears flood the despair inside me. When we leave each other, an unusual silence hangs heavy in the air.

CHAPTER 30

Next day Meriam surprises me with a phone call at work. I'm in the middle of preparing the menu for the coming week, the afternoon before taking my vacation.

"Something happened. Can you come right away?" Meriam says, her voice shaking.

I try to find out what it is.

"I don't want to talk about it by phone. Let's meet in the parking lot of Star Market in Cambridge."

My heart panics all the way to the store thinking Sam probably knows about us. I was expecting this to happen any time. The anticipation of confrontations, the avalanche of the unknown is overwhelming. What should I do now? Stand like an Eagle Boy Scout and say, "I love your wife. Of course, it's pure love. Yes, we made love."

In the parking lot, Meriam is waiting for me. "We had a horrible fight about Esther," her grip on my hand is tight.

"What about Esther?"

"For months now, Esther has been moping around because Riyad never tells her, not even once, that he loves her. I think it is the revenge of unrequited love, the humiliation of a modern woman. Riyad took her to bed faster than her mind could handle. Besides, Esther is more complex than you think. Sam is fed up with Riyad, and started ranting about how he's deceiving his daughter."

"And me? Is he fed up with me too?"

"No, no. He truly likes you, loves you, in his words. You are a best friend, his chef, on and on. He says his restaurant will collapse without you."

"How did your fight end?"

"Sameer, it was horrible. I've never fought with Sam like this before. He wouldn't calm down. He was yelling at me." Meriam is overcome by tears, a sob the size of an ocean wave takes her under. I wait helplessly for her to continue.

She regains her composure. "I think it's better to change location and go for a drive."

"Where's Sam?"

"I left him at home."

"Where does he think you are?"

"I packed a suitcase. I told him I'm going to visit my parents."

"Are you?"

"Yes, I couldn't stay at home tonight. Sam needs to cool off."

In the back seat of the Continental I notice Meriam's suitcase and a bag not completely zipped.

"Did you take a sedative?" I ask.

"No, do you have any?"

"No sedatives will help when love is at stake." I have a knack for empty platitudes when I'm utterly confused.

I caress Meriam reassuringly, but my arm is heavy with worry.

"Tomorrow is your vacation. Come down to Connecticut, come and visit me. I need you."

"I'll phone my assistant at the Oasis, I'll go with you today. I'll drive you to your parents. It's only a couple of hours. Do you think Sam knows about us?"

"If he does he didn't show it," Meriam says.

I call the Oasis and tell them that I am taking vacation one day earlier. I leave word for Sam. Meriam calls Vera. I drop off my car. We drive south to Connecticut. Martin is home on vacation, and Vera says she is always happy to see us.

I saw a silver Viking bowl in Copenhagen, large enough to hold a goat, ornate with obscure symbols, used for sacrificial blood of humans. And what about all the maidens thrown in the Nile? The Nile is still muddy, and Egyptians continue sacrificing. In modern times, sacrifice is staged inside prisons with less fanfare and stripped of rituals. The cries of maidens were drowned in rituals and chants.

Meriam shakes off my anxiety. "Where have we been all this time?"

"We must be the last breed of dreamers," I say.

We arrive. Vera senses the unknown and insists that I stay overnight. Meriam, still tense, looks at me entreatingly. I agree, hoping I may be able to calm her. I need calming myself, for I can see Vera looking at me closely. To my disappointment, Vera takes Meriam to the garden, I'm sure for debriefing. Martin steers me to his office. His favorite topic is still on his mind, the collapse of Western Civilization.

"The president wants to invest in more technology. God save us."

My mind is totally blocked to Marin's intellectual games.

"The political future is dismal. It's like a Russian doll, it opens to more miniatures of the same kind." Martin sits in his worn leather chair, smoking his pipe. "On top of that, my eyesight is failing and my deafness gets worse with old age."

"Where do you expect salvation to come from, if at all? Bangladesh, Mecca or Israel?" I ask him cynically.

Martin overlooks my cynicism. "I had an argument with Richard about this question. I told him I believe in Israel. Richard had the audacity to tell me, 'Israel lost her purity, a nun became a whore. The utmost you expect from her is to serve her client's groins.' Can you imagine Richard telling me that?" I was shocked. "I sat thinking afterwards, with Vera, where did we fail him along the way? All those days in Hebrew school, in youth organizations." Then, realizing suddenly he's talking to a Palestinian, he says, "Sorry, Sameer, I forgot. I always feel you are one of us."

Early the next morning Meriam wakes me with a cup of coffee and slides next to me, her body shaking.

"I couldn't sleep," she tells me.

"I couldn't either." I try to find out more about what happened between Meriam and Sam. We go over it several times. She finally tells me the real problem, the real reason.

"Sam wants to have a baby. The fight went from Esther to Riyad to a baby. It was so awful."

"What stopped the fight?"

"He was frightened I'd leave him. I said I needed a break and left."

Looking out the window I see the faint sun cutting through the morning fog. I'm worried that Martin and Vera may find us together. Meriam assures me they never deviate from their morning routine, which doesn't involve us. It's going to be difficult for me to look Vera in the eyes. Strange that I didn't mind Vera's eyes last time. I was dizzy. Euphoria numbs social concerns.

"Did you tell them much about your fight with Sam?"

"No that would make things worse. They never approved of my marriage. Dad would only become self-righteous. Mom questioned me last night. She knows me too well, but she never gets anything out of me before I'm ready." Meriam tightens her grip on my hand. "This is not what you had in mind for your vacation."

"The trouble is that Riyad has the momentum of a running buffalo. His convictions keep him looking a hundred yards ahead of the immediate traps. I tried to call him late last night, but there was no answer."

After breakfast I attempt to maneuver an easy exit. Vera and Martin suggest I stay longer, saying they'll invite Meriam's brother over. I decline.

"You've got to see Nicole," Vera tells me.

"The hope of the future," Martin says sighing, having the previous night condemned, judged, and disposed of the world situation.

"I'd love to see Nicole," Meriam says. "I'll give her a big hug from you." She is in a wide V-necked, cotton top and attractive blue shorts.

Do Martin and Vera notice the flow of intimacy between us? Martin

- - absolutely not. But Vera does have sensitivity and intuition. I feel she sees through me.

Meriam insists I should drive her Continental back. I insist on taking the bus. I don't feel like driving. Illusions are shredded. I hug Meriam good-bye and look at her. I detect trepidation in her loving eyes. The murkiness of an unknown future lurks like a shutter on the surface. They take me to the bus terminal.

CHAPTER 31

Back at the Oasis, I find out that Sam is on vacation too. He rushed out to start his own vacation as soon as he heard I was starting my vacation a day early.

"Vacations are contagious," Judy announces, "Sam can't be reached for ten days at least."

I keep calling Meriam in Connecticut but our telephone conversations range from long silences broken by few words to indignation about how absurd all of this is. My calls are being off-set by calls from Sam.

I remember that I have always gained peace in churches - - from their thick walls, their high ceilings, their coolness and serenity. I remember reading about a silent retreat, literally silent. Residents go there for meditation, no talking allowed. It's in central Massachusetts, in the midst of a rural area; it's called Josephine House.

I phone them for details. A low whisper answers, asking me to write them explaining my needs. They prefer to respond in writing. The spoken word is agitating. I whisper back that I'm in dire need of silence.

"Then come," the woman tells me. I throw a few clothes together, and some food.

I'm traveling light, with a heavy heart.

All of my American experience comes to a halting jam. Suddenly the problems of Sam and Meriam, my feelings for my family, and the question of what am I doing in the U.S. crash like tidal waves. I need silence. I take the Hippie Christ with me, pens and paper, and drive to Route 31 where Josephine House is located.

Have you ever been in total silence? It's terrifying.

A different world rests outside the Boston area, less populated, less heady. In the midst of my anxieties, glimpses of fields and maple trees brighten the drive. That there is a world with yellow wildflowers and relaxed countryside comes as a revelation. In the city the seasons are mostly felt in waves of excessive humidity or heat, of rain or snow, and nature is adulterated and subdued under the thumb of concrete. In the Galilee it is silver green olive leaves, spreading over deeper green fig trees and waving golden wheat ready for harvest.

I stop for lunch at a roadside country diner. Far from Boston, country people are closer to the forest. They appear unpruned, bending and growing in all directions. Women come obese, their breasts weighing on dinner tables, the folds of their tummies in their way, with fashionless but functional eyeglasses and big wedding rings. As soon as they talk, you notice that they care, they are kind.

Those diners on the road show me a different American. Behind the soot there is marble, just the opposite from the city. They drive each other places, for they can always count on a car not starting, on one woman who doesn't drive. They bring their children and their neighbor's children to the diner, and they talk about basic survival, the roosters and the hens, the husbands and their work, the beans they are going to pick this weekend, how they hate to drive because they get lost, and they hate to go to the city. The city is usually a town larger than their own, nearby, not Boston. Women wave their knives spreading butter as if they were painting a house. The simplicity and the warmth of Brueghel's country figures. The country's the only place I feel technology is lagging behind people.

Why do I stay in the U.S.? My link has always been anchored through love, through a woman, first Christine, then Meriam. Am I Americanized? Are there patches of American coloring showing all over my body, my accent? Are my problems reduced to the mediocrity of typical immigrant adjustment?

But America is a grand, hospitable country, living on the surface of one change, in anticipation of the next. I spark with American pride when I think that America can go through a Watergate and survive. That they could have dumped Nixon and forgiven him with time. The country that once agreed to be represented by Kissinger's heavy German accent as a Secretary of State fills me with pride for its inner flexibility and good-heartedness. Would France have ever allowed a Mitterrand with an English accent?

America is a great country. I'm lucky I was able to see a country acting on its destiny. I saw it liberating blacks, women, and doing it with the least bloodshed. Could I just tear off my attachment to this country like an orange peel? Never.

A large truck passes me on the road, loaded with trees, full grown trees with their roots in containers, tied closely around their trunks. I'm like one of those trees, having no control over my destiny.

I drive through small towns, people everywhere in T-shirts and jeans and shorts. Living for change, they dress for it. The houses are ready for change. They can be folded, added, or rebuilt. You do it in bricks or prefab, but not in stone. Stones preserve. Pyramids rest on the chest of centuries, containers of the past.

My mind finds temporary relief, the relief of the dam opening, the relief of the overspill. I drift into sanctuaries.

While driving, I stop and find diversion in another country diner along the way. Customers sit, confidently discussing politics. They can call their Congressman, criticize their government and laugh at the same time. What a far cry from the mock front and humorless respectability that dictators portray. People are not allowed to mention their names without adding, "The Loved," "The Great Guardian," "The Watchful Father," "The Intelligent and Compassionate," even if their beards cover VD sores. This goes on while the screams of arrested citizens are choked inside prison walls. Mental slavery parades in pretentious colors.

Would we be able to tailor a different Palestine? Can we create the Palestine I carry inside me, peaceful and harmonious, where the families are together and happy, where Palestine is a democracy, where there is an ombudsman that listens to grievances, where there are judges that abide by justice? Palestine should be justice. Cut the sentimentality, Sameer,

I tell myself.

I know dreams are stronger when they are handed down from generations. Children in refugee camps who never saw Palestine see it today through the rosy nostalgia of their parents. The dream has become a passion, both romantic and mythical. Their struggle is starting to read like a Greek legend.

My drive winds through back country.

Women stand behind tables at yard sales facing no customers.

A sign says a "faith healer" is conducting a session in the local auditorium this evening. From the shelves of the religious pharmacy you can pick and choose your personalized formula of sweetener. Jesus the Scientist, the Universalist, the healer, the evangelist. You can be slain by the spirit, saved with donations, healed by touching a radio heating up with religious steam. Whatever sells is valid. Christ the salesman is on the shelves, and anything that sells must be true.

Should I go back to the healing session? Would He see through the pores, the agony? The last time I was curious about healers, I attended a crusade and joined the masses who walked down to the platform to be Born Again. Two ministers administered the rites to me. I read a passage from the Bible. That was it. They congratulated me on my "spiritual insurance."

They asked where I was from, and when I said Nazareth, the Holy Land, they didn't understand why a man of Nazareth needed to be reborn in Boston, Massachusetts. But I had been given their insurance policy. They tried to collect on it afterwards. I never sent donations. At the time I was more in need of donations than they were.

Anything that sells must be true. And here I am defying the recipe, trying to cure myself, by myself and not from the shelves.

CHAPTER 32

Josephine House is hidden in a pond of silence. All the echoes subside as I approach. Both noise of machine and man freeze like icicles. The house is a large mansion transformed into Still Life.

I find a welcoming note on the kitchen table. I can use anything in the kitchen. My room is waiting and ready. Ready for what?

Good used furniture is scattered in calm comfort around a fireplace in the living room. There is a sense that things do not move here, that people and objects hang motionless in suspense, elevated with no gravity. Bookshelves are lined along the side - - prayers, philosophy, meditation. It's a setting for miracles. I sink in a comfortable chair, stretch my feet forward and pray for one miracle that could cleanse my eyes, my soul, my heart, so that I can see clearer. So that I can see.

In the midst of the silence of Josephine House life bounces from all sides. Distant corners of the past flash.

Christmas. Christmas dinner. Father laughing. Mother happy, my brother joking, we are enjoying the meal. Mother is proud we are already grown up. Happy, happy memories. White tablecloths and huge platters heaped with stuffed green squash, stuffed chicken, the aroma of nutmeg, cinnamon, rice and pine nuts, hearty sweet wine I was allowed, and a sense of gentle excitement that everyone in Nazareth is celebrating. There will be a flow of guests coming to wish us "Merry Christmas" from shortly after lunch all the way through midnight. Relatives will come, festive in Christmas suits, their kids holding onto the coins they received in the morning, dreaming of endless combinations they can buy.

Security in a shell. Mother and Father stretch to seal all corners. We are sealed in happiness, incubated in warmth. How did I get cast out? How did I fly so far? My wings must be filled with scars, smoke and burn marks. I don't call up those memories. They call on me and leave me in fear. I have a strange feeling I'm communicating with Father from where I sit.

I doze off. I wake up back to my own nightmare. What's happening to Meriam? What's happening to Sam, Meriam and me? But there are no phones, no radios, no television in Josephine House. I am left with myself and terrified by the encounter, by suppressed truth surfacing. I know the questions. The answers still escape me.

Why do memories sound silly when you write them down? Memories lose their fresh aroma like frozen bread. I try to breathe life into memories of times I spent with friends reading poetry on the rocks of the Galilee. Talking, talking, and then watching the sunset. Long evenings of talk, of food, and drinks in Arab villages. I cannot bring it all back. I can only create a longing for a once peaceful past.

Funny how innocence is entwined with happiness, entwined with ignorance, just like a peaceful rock nestled on a bed of wild flowers, visited by raindrops and birds, settled over a nest of scorpions.

The past spurts through me, up and out, unannounced. I pray that if geysers spurt murkiness, it will be short lived.

I long for my mother, my brother, my cousins, my friends. I'm tempted to go back. I envision myself in Nazareth and imagine America carried within me like a nostalgic dream. Meriam is like a magnet in my helpless brain.

I jolt against the question of will. Can I stop seeing Meriam? Centuries of traditions, of morality anchored within my family, carried from generation to generation, haunt me. Do I need exorcism? I should walk to the Trappist Monastery nearby and ask for a spiritual cleansing. The monks must have gone through it.

At midnight in Josephine House the silence is draped in darkness. Here in this shrine I am out of reach, but for me the silence is filled with oracles, and the unknown remains bittersweet.

In the silence I drift back to Nazareth.

Abu Riyad, Riyad's Father, always telling me, "You are like my son,

Sameer. You and Riyad are brothers." How do brothers move so far apart? What should I tell Um Riyad, his mother, when she brings sweet tea and toast with goat cheese and sits just long enough to wish me luck and pray that Allah continues to protect me? Allah's protection. Is Allah still on the premises?

St. Joseph's Abbey is near Josephine House. I walk over at 3 a.m. for Gregorian chanting. The brothers march into the chapel in gold robes. About forty of them singing, praying, a few lit candles and long shadows dance wildly around in my imagination, around their life and mine, my escape and theirs. There is peace in the cool ceiling of the night. Is that peace? How do brothers look in broad daylight?

I go back to Josephine House. There is no other soul here. My life continues to parade through an erratic kaleidoscope.

I'm hoping I can see the landscape of the past. I'm hoping if I stand on a remote mountaintop, I can see below. But below is haze and the scene forever changes. Do I need forty days in the wilderness in order to see?

I'm starting to taste the bitter flavor of betrayal. Will Meriam betray me with Sam?

I stand in my room and pray. I go to the nearby abbey, stand to the side of the chapel, and pray and entreat whoever is there to have mercy on all of us.

At night my Hippie Christ glares in red sunset lights, "Don't move too fast on things not under your control."

"What shall I do?" I ask him. I must do something. "You don't answer me when I need you," I scream and shatter the silence.

I take walks in the hilly countryside. The old acorns are scattered below oak trees, sun and rain keep the luscious green bursting and bright. Endless blue jays and robins, endless barn swallows parading on electric lines waiting patiently for the first rays of the warm sun, all in tune with light and darkness.

Maybe man is lucky that he can roam beyond the span of his worries. A deep awe and love for a beautiful universe grips me in the midst of tragedy.

I can't remember whether I have been at Josephine House three or four days. Like most problems, I seem to work out an acceptance rather than a solution. Sam is absent, Meriam is absent.

Would you marry me, Meriam? No, you can't build a fast ship from wreckage.

In farewell, I touch the corners of Josephine House and leave it, laced with tranquility. I try to find rest in the eye of the storm. I almost forget to pack my Hippie Christ, then lay him by my side and drive back.

CHAPTER 33

Back in Watertown I face bills.

I phone Meriam. "I missed you," I say with the first breath. "When will I see you?"

"I'm not sure."

"I thought you were, before I left."

"Sameer, try to understand."

"Are you coming back?"

"Sameer," Meriam whispers, "I thought things over."

"Yes, what things?"

"Us," Meriam says. "I thought about us and I think it's better if you don't come down to Westport."

"Of course," I say, my pride slightly hurt. "Why aren't you coming up?"

"Sam wants me to stay here until he returns." Meriam sounds as if she's in Westport on a vacation, not in refuge. I'm puzzled that she's complying with Sam's request.

"Is there anything new? Did anything happen?"

"You know how much I love you," Meriam says. "I literally shake wanting to see you, but I don't feel very well. I feel like I have the flu."

"Well," I urge gently.

"It's much better if we don't see each other until Sam returns. It's one less complication."

"I feel I am trapped."

"What do you mean?"

"I mean I'm trapped with indecision. I don't know what's becoming of us. I'm trapped at work and with Sam."

It's a long time before I hear Meriam's voice. "Sameer, she says, "there's something else I need to tell you."

"Yes?" I ask her.

"I've decided I want to have a child."

"Are you pregnant?"

"I don't know. I hope not. It's the first time Sam ever wanted one. It's strange."

Meriam hangs up.

I'm afraid Meriam is pregnant and has decided to stay with Sam. If it's my child, I want to feel the same bond that tied me to my father.

"Who is the father?" I ask my Hippie Christ.

He stares back at me, a twinkle of a smile around his lips. "Some children are born from unknown fathers," he says.

CHAPTER 34

Sam returns to the Oasis.

"Sam, I can't work here anymore."

"Don't be a fool - - nobody will pay you better - - you can't leave us just like that. After all we've been to you, and you to us."

Is he playing a poker game? He probably assumes I know, and he's playing his hand to perfection.

"What shall I tell Meriam?" Sam yells.

I hold my breath and tell him what he least expects. "I love Meriam."

Sam glares at me, then roars back, "Why? Why do you have to tell me?"

"I can't stand the dishonesty any longer, yours or mine," I scream back.

Sam explodes. "Your God damned honesty, your retarded values, your screwed up sense of integrity. What about me?" he asks. "What about my feelings for Meriam? You're offering this confession for your own sake, not for me. How do you think we can live together after this? I've known Meriam for fifteen years. You come in and try to screw it all up." Sam's grip on the chair in front of him is menacing. "Meriam is staying with me. If you think Meriam's going to leave Newton and go with you in a two-decker apartment in Watertown, which I own, you don't know the ABCs about women. If it takes you one century to know other women, it will take you two to know Meriam."

Sam storms out of the room then returns screaming, "What exactly do you expect me to do? Kill you, then kill her? You're a fool, Sameer. You spoiled everything - - the three of us were managing so well. I kept you all this time because I care about Meriam. I love Meriam more than your self-righteous mind can comprehend. I kept you because I love her and you make her happy, but you're tearing all this to shreds. Do me a favor, clear out of my restaurant and my life. Don't tell her, don't see her,

I'll manage all the rest."

Sam's screaming freezes all action at the Oasis. Lava bursts from him, yellow and red in anger and venom. The frenzy of his anger numbs me. His rage blocks his curiosity - - he doesn't ask me if we made love. Let this torment him.

I'm thrown out of the Oasis and out of Sam's life.

When I call Meriam to explain I didn't tell Sam about us, Meriam simply asks, "Please, Sameer, make this your last telephone call."

I can't stay in Sam's apartment in Watertown any longer. I sit in front of my Hippie Christ.

"You have a long face - - you remind me of the Last Supper," my Hippie Christ tells me.

"I have no patience with your metaphors, parables and fables," I answer.

"You're trying to become a tragedy."

Impatient, I ask, "I lost my home, the woman I love, my country. What is left?"

"Hope," He says.

"Don't patronize me. Hope you say. Where, when, how?" I stare him in the eyes, but Christ fades into the painting.

CHAPTER 35

My U-Haul rattles behind me again, a mourning melody for lost love.

Flags fly proudly over manicured lawns. The earth means so much to us, why can't we have a bit of it? Our own. The flags fly proudly as I drive west. Americans own a piece of land under the flag, and it stretches to the sky.

I find a job as a cook in Worcester, Massachusetts and move into a studio apartment overlooking Holy Cross College. Both my employer and my landlord have Greek names and Greek accents.

Pizzeria Acropolis is not the Oasis. We serve Gyros and pizza, and my landlord has religious pictures and icons all over the place.

Months have passed, my boxes are still packed. The summer was filled with anxiety, the fall with grief. The shutters of depression keep the colorful New England fall from filtering inside me. In the front yard there's a maple tree already stripped of its leaves, dormant, ready for the cold. My tears are frozen inside me.

I unpack my Hippie Christ from one of the sealed boxes, dust Him, hang Him and apologize. I find Him a prominent spot and sit by the window, pen in hand, with an empty pad of paper. I'm looking through the window to the cold Jesuit buildings of Holy Cross College.

I read a letter I got from Christine, reminiscent of a solid, honest love. She's got her tenure and is getting married.

It's raining. I feel guilty that I betrayed Sam with Meriam. I miss Meriam. I start to write. I write that "I am deeply, deeply sorry." Shall I send this to Sam or Meriam? I add, "I want to see you," and send it to Meriam.

In Nazareth, out-of-season rain is barakah, a blessing. It's a good omen. Rain is invoked by prayer. It's linked to God. In Nazareth, during a drought, people walk in long processions repeating simple chants to the saints - - to Mary, Joseph, and to Jesus, praying for rain. Moslems and Christians walk side-by-side, kadis and clergy, men and women. Drums set the tone for echoing chants. We start the procession at Mary's well and go down the main street. The earth cracks in thirst. The dust is blazing hot ashes. The melody of the procession hypnotizes people, even children calm down. They feel in contact with divinity.

"Rain is barakah min Allah." A blessing from God. Is there a blessing for Nazareth?

I ask my Hippie Christ at night, "Is there an end to all of this?"

"I hope so," my Hippie Christ answers, His eyes filling with tears.

"But you said there's Hope."

"There's Hope."